MY

STORIES FROM
NEW EDEN

Ogre

HUSBAND

LYONNE RILEY

Introduction

Maddie is one of only one hundred humans remaining, living behind the high walls of the New Eden preserve in order to protect her from the monsters that rule the world. Though Maddie longs for love, all her attempts at trial marriages have failed—leaving her wondering if she's lovable enough to find her happily ever after.

Egorr the ogre wants a companion in life. When he applies for Maddie through the Human Companion program, they hit it off right away. Egorr is a gentle giant who adores Maddie's good humor, and soon, they agree to a trial marriage.

But Egorr is big in more ways than one. When their first attempt at intimacy doesn't go as planned, the two must figure out how to navigate love, sex, and marriage together. Can Maddie truly open her heart when she's afraid of being hurt again?

Content Warnings

May contain spoilers

- Graphic depictions of sex
- Unintentional sexual injury (perineal tear)
- Light BDSM
- Stretching and stuffing
- Use of sex toys

Chapter One

"All I'm asking for is a chair!" Tears are building behind my eyes, making them sting, as I try to get across once again what my basic needs are. "I just want a chair, Shisek. The table isn't any good to me without a chair."

"Humans," he says, flexing his long shadowy claws as he frowns. "First it was a bed. Then a couch. Now a chair?" He lets out that disapproving hiss I've come to despise.

"Yes! Those are all things we need!" I'm trying so hard not to cry, not to give Shisek the gratification of letting him know how much he hurts me, but it's biting at my cheeks with a painful intensity. "I can't eat on the couch every day."

I don't think I've been comfortable for even a moment since I moved in to do a trial marriage with Shisek. I knew he was a shadow demon, and shadow demons don't need much in the way of furniture given how they can shift without a physical form through the world. His home is somewhere between dimensions, so it's not easy to get furniture delivered, either.

I knew all this, but I had hoped he would try harder to accommodate me, to make his house a home for me as the trial marriage rules stipulated. But the only thing he'd had ready for me when I moved in was a bed, as if that's all a human needs to be happy.

Now I'm starting to believe Shisek didn't want me at all, and he's just afraid of being lonely. He should be, given how grouchy and rude he's been since I came here. Sometimes I think he applied for a human companion because even his own kind won't tolerate him.

Shisek's glowing red eyes narrow. "I can't afford to buy so many superfluous things," he says, his form shifting as he moves across the shadowy room.

"You should have thought of that before you applied for a human companion," I growl back.

This isn't the first time we've fought over this subject—and many other subjects, too. Probably the most painful time was when I asked if we could have sex, and Shisek told me we had "some things to work out first."

I should have known that was the end, but I clung onto hope. I wanted this happily ever after so badly, and I wanted the freedom that Shisek gives me out in the world. He can shift into any size and shape he likes, and his great big fangs are enough to scare off any monsters who might want to hurt or eat me. It made him the perfect choice for a partner, or so I thought.

Not that we've gone much of anywhere. Shisek is also a homebody, which means I haven't even been to the grocery store. He simply orders what I want and picks it up on his way home from work. I'm trapped all day in this shadow house, unable to even step out the front door unless Shisek is with me to guide me back to the physical plane.

"Yes," Shisek finally answers. "I am coming to realize that applying for you was a mistake, Maddie."

The words are enough to send a shock of pure fury surging

through my body. My tears break free at last, and they stream down my face as I shoot up from the couch.

"Then take me back!" I want to just reach out and grab him, shake him by his collar, but he's carefully dematerialized himself. "Take me home!"

It turns out that was all I needed to say. That night, I pack my bags and Shisek silently leads me to the entrance to the shadow realm. There, his car is waiting for us, and he drives me back to New Eden without a word.

"Good riddance," I mutter as he pulls away, leaving me alone on the curb with my bags. But I can't mask all my heartbreak with anger. When the car is gone, I sink down to my knees on the sidewalk and cry until one of the guards hears me. He helps me carry my things inside the high walls of the preserve, back to the place I thought I'd finally left for the last time.

Now here I am, embarrassed by my failure and trapped in a prison once more.

In the following days, I try not to let on how much it hurts that things fell apart with Shisek. I don't want people to think I'm fragile, to know how much it aches to be sent home. I hug my parents, smiling, telling them how the breakup was mutual and amicable.

But my best friend, Celeste, must sense that everything isn't quite as I pretend, because she comes up with all sorts of activities for us to do together. She demands that I help her with the garden during the day, and in the evenings, she invites me over to cook and play cards. I'm usually the one who insists on our little friend group hanging out, but she's taken up the mantle of urging us all to get together and do distracting activities.

In the last few months, I've gotten a few new applications from monsters who are interested in me. I've ignored them, but tonight Celeste insisted that we sit down at the table together to shuffle through them, looking for the one who could be my perfect match.

I have very low hopes.

"What about this guy?" she asks, sliding over an application. The picture attached to it features a centaur, big and beefy in the shoulders and chest, with a handsome face and a gorgeous, dapple grey coat on his lower half. He's beautiful, I have to admit, and is probably hung like a... well, like a horse.

"How does that work?" I ask, cocking my head at the photograph. "Does he mount me?" I try to imagine this, and I wonder if it would even fit.

Celeste furrows her brow. "I don't know. It does seem like it might be complicated."

I push the application away and drop my head down on the table. It's not really about the sex—though that is very important to me. It's the idea of offering my heart again that haunts me, hoping that some centaur won't stomp on it the way Shisek did.

I was so thrilled the day I packed up my things, absolutely sure that this was my chance to find my happily ever after. And maybe the problem is that I was too eager, too blinded by my rose-colored glasses to see the truth about Shisek. Because truly, I hate it here in New Eden. There aren't many humans left in the world, and those that are? We're trapped behind these high walls to keep us safe from monsters that roam the world outside. It's a boring existence. There's so much out there in the world to do and see, and I could never see it unless I left.

So I was willing to overlook the red flags if it meant freedom.

Celeste pats my back. "What's really wrong?" she asks. "There's something bothering you."

It's hard to hide from my best friend, who knows me better than even my own mother. My parents haven't asked more than a couple of questions since I came back, but Celeste seems to have sussed out what I'm hiding.

The tears come to my eyes before I can stop them.

"What if no one wants me?" I ask, wiping my face. "What if I never get chosen by someone who I want to choose, too?" I push all the applications away, scattering them across the ground.

Maybe I'm too much. Maybe I'm too energetic, or demanding, or needy. Maybe Shisek was my best chance at love and I blew it by asking for that chair.

Celeste gasps. "Maddie!" She scoots her chair closer and wraps me up in a hug. "All of these monsters want you. They wouldn't have applied for you otherwise."

"But I don't want any of them!" My tears are flowing faster now. "I can't end up with another Shisek. It would break me, Celeste."

Sometimes when it's dark, I think no one will ever love me the way I want to be loved. I want freedom as much as I want companionship. I want to experience something as average and normal as grocery shopping. I want to make love, and have meals together, and cuddle up on the couch for a silly TV show with my companion in life.

Celeste wipes my cheek with her thumb. "You won't end up with another Shisek. You know what warning signs to look for now, and you know what you want. You just have to be a little patient until the right one comes along."

"I guess so," I say, sniffling. "But I'm tired of waiting."

She nods. "I know. You want to be swept off your feet. And you deserve that."

When I've cooled off a little, I notice there's just one application left on the table after my tantrum.

NAME: EGORR

There's no last name—just "Egorr."

SPECIES: OGRE

I've never had an ogre apply for me before. His photo is... unusual. He's almost too big for the camera to capture, with a huge green body, and a big round head. He has no hair, and massive tusks protrude from his lower jaw, nearly curling up to his brows.

At first, I think he's the opposite of handsome with that squashed-looking nose and small eyes. But something in his smile, which looks awkward and a little forced, speaks to me. It's like he's holding in what he really is and putting on the face he thinks I would want.

I'm curious what's behind that smile.

An ogre would certainly keep me safe out in the world, being eight feet tall and bigger than most other monsters we might encounter, save for giants. Immediately I think of how big his cock must be, and my eyes go wide.

"Maddie?" Celeste asks, her gaze following mine to the application. She quirks an eyebrow. "An ogre?"

I trace his smile in the photograph before realizing I should probably read the rest of the application.

OCCUPATION: SOFTWARE DEVELOPER

An ogre who programs computers? Huh. I don't know why I expected him to be a lumberjack, or maybe a pro weightlifter. I read further on.

"My life is pretty quiet," his personal statement reads. "I want to share it with someone who I can come home to every day. I have a lot of love to give, and I just haven't been able to find the person I want to give it to."

My heart twists in my chest. I know just what he means. I have so much devotion inside me, so much desire and longing, and nowhere for it to go. I want someone who has just as much to offer me in return. I want to love and feel loved completely.

"What do you think?" asks Celeste. "Can you give it another try with someone else?"

The more I look at the picture, the more I can imagine Egorr being handsome. With just that tiny glimpse of what he is inside, I could see myself being attracted to him, huge tusks and all.

Maybe Celeste is right, and I can't judge Egorr based on Shisek. This ogre is a whole separate, different person, and there's a chance he could be just what I'm looking for.

I check through the rest of the application, which contains all the notes from the resident director during the vetting process. She's written down things like, "Very considerate," "a little forgetful," and "already has plans for decorating Maddie's bedroom."

My heart swells just the smallest amount. An ogre certainly has furniture already, so that's a plus. And I have a fantastic memory, so we should complement each other well.

"All right," I say with a sigh. "I'll ask him to meet."

"Good." Celeste's smile is radiant and encouraging. "I think you're brave to try again."

I swat away her compliment. "Now I just have to figure out what to wear!"

Chapter Two

I'm a bundle of nerves after informing the resident director that I'd like to meet Egorr, but I try to play it cool. I spend two whole days mulling over what to wear for our meeting, and even get my mother's input, though she has atrocious taste—but it's not like Celeste's is much better. I'm on my own when it comes to picking something out.

Eventually I decide on a modest blue blouse with a matching polka-dot skirt, and my favorite blue flats. Hopefully Egorr doesn't think I'm too overdone.

I can't think like that. If I don't want a repeat of Shisek, I have to be my real self. I have to ask for what I want and need, and let my potential partner decide if he's interested or not. Egorr sounds like a nice guy, but if how I dress is going to be a deal-breaker, I'd rather know now.

Before our meeting, I find out what I can about ogres. They tend to be solitary, or so the internet says, and they build their homes in mountains and hills. Once married, they stay with their partner for life. They typically eat a lot to sustain their big bodies but only need a meal once or twice a day. I wonder how that would work when I need three squares daily.

After reading the whole article, I'm more worried about our differences than ever. Would I fit into his life? Would he need to buy extra furniture to accommodate my much smaller size? Would he want to travel, to do things and explore the world, if he's cooped up in his den alone all the time?

Celeste comes over that morning to bring me breakfast and give me a pep talk, which is funny to me coming from someone who won't even look at her own applications. She busies about, dropping encouraging words as I put on some light makeup. I want to disguise the bags under my eyes, but not hide who I am. I'm grateful to have her there, and before I head to the meeting, she gives me a big hug.

"Something will work out for you," she says. "I know it in my heart."

It's cheesy, but I hope she's right. I want to find my forever person.

I try to gather up all my confidence before I step into the meeting room. I'm pretty and smart, and I know what I want. I'm not willing to accept half measures any longer. No more Shiseks.

I don't know if I believe all of it in my heart, but I'm going to pretend I do.

Steeling myself, I head inside.

When I open the door and peer through, I find Egorr's already inside and talking with the resident director. He's gigantic. Like, really, *really* big. His clothes are huge, too, and seem to be barely holding in his big chest and belly. His tusks are even longer in real life than they looked in his picture, but his head is just as empty of hair.

Samantha spots me and says brightly, "Hi, Maddie!"

Egorr turns around, and when he sees me, his mouth falls open.

"Oh," is all that comes out. Samantha gestures for me to come in, so I do, letting the door fall closed behind me. Egorr hasn't stopped staring, and I wonder if I have something on my face.

"I'll leave you two alone," the resident director says, giving me a broad smile. Then she lets herself out, and Egorr and I are by ourselves.

I decide to jump right into it. "Hi!" I say cheerily, holding out my hand. "It's nice to meet you, Egorr."

The ogre blinks a few times, like he's just realized where we are and what we're doing.

"Hello," he says, and his voice is incredibly deep, like a didgeridoo. "Thank you for meeting me, Maddie."

He shakes my hand, and his utterly dwarfs mine, his palm swallowing up my fingers. Then he releases me, and Egorr gestures politely to one of the couches. When I sit down, he finds his own seat on the couch opposite of me, so I feel like I'm going to a counseling session.

"I should be the one thanking you for meeting *me*," I say with a nervous laugh. "Thanks for, um, applying. And then coming all the way out here."

Though Egorr's smile had looked a little forced in his application photo, this time when he smiles, the radiance of it takes me by surprise. His bulky lower lip pulls up on the sides, his tusks rising high on his face. He has such a big, wide mouth, and his eyes crinkle so adorably that it sets me at ease right away.

"I was really happy to get the call," he says, that booming

voice sending a little shock down my spine. "I've been hoping for a while I'd hear from you."

"Really?" Now I feel terrible about how long I took to respond. I was just so weighed down with Shisek that I'd put it off, not even thinking about the monsters on the other side of the applications who might be waiting to hear from me.

"Of course." Egorr's smile softens. "When I heard nothing, I got worried I might never get picked."

"Oh, sorry." I drop my eyes to the floor. "I should have accepted or declined sooner. I just..." I shake off the flood of sadness that washes over me. "I've been busy, that's all!"

He nods. "I understand. I'm glad we get to meet now." Egorr sits up straighter and adjusts the collar of his dress shirt. It's clearly a little uncomfortable around his thick neck. "It's not like I was doing much."

"So you work in computers," I say, deciding to turn the conversation toward getting to know Egorr better. "Tell me about that?"

He tenses up, like this subject makes him nervous. "Not a lot to say, I suppose. I go to the office, I write software code and hunt down bugs, then I come home." That wide smile has fallen off his face. "It's not very exciting."

"I think it's exciting," I say. I've never met someone who works on computers, and I'm not all that good at using them myself. "What kind of software?"

He blinks. "Oh. Well." Egorr clears his throat. "You know the CGI in movies and games?"

I nod. "Like when something blows up?"

"Exactly. I work on the software that other companies use to make computer-generated effects like that."

This actually *is* very exciting.

"So your stuff has been in movies?"

Egorr chortles. "I guess you could say that, in an indirect way. They use the tools I've helped develop."

"So..." I find I've been twirling my hair in my nervousness, and I drop my hand immediately. "What do you do for fun, Egorr?"

The happiness falls from his face. "Oh, um. Not a ton. I play video games in the evenings, usually, to relax after work. But sometimes I work late, then just go home and go to bed."

I cock my head. "Is that part of the job? Do your coworkers work late, too?"

Egorr shrugs. "No, they all have families they go home to, so they're always eager to leave right at five o'clock."

I can hear the words he isn't saying: *But I'm not.* He doesn't have a family of his own, though if I gathered anything from his application, it's that he wants one more than anything else.

"If you had someone at home, would you still work late?" It's an important question, because I don't want to be left home alone all day long. I expect I'll have to entertain myself most of the time, but it's not worth it if we can't see each other in the evenings.

"Oh, of course not!" Egorr's brows are high on his forehead. "I would ditch work as soon as possible if I had, um... *someone* at home."

I think he means me, and it makes my heart beat a little faster.

But there is a sticking point. He wants a *family*. I can't give him children, not as we're different species. Is that something he wants?

"Can I ask a blunt question?" I say. Not that I know how to ask in any other way.

He cocks his head. "Sure."

"Why not a lady ogre?"

Egorr's eyes go even wider, and I don't think that's what he was expecting me to say. His mouth opens like he's about to answer, but then he closes it again and looks away, his green cheeks turning a darker color.

"What?" I lean forward. I know humans are incredibly desirable among monsters. We're cute, we're helpless, we're small. Whatever it is about us, they want a taste. So I need to know why Egorr applied for me specifically—and I don't want it to be because I'm small and cute and maybe a good hole for his cock.

"Well," Egorr says, swallowing hard, "I'm not, um... I'm not very interested. In other ogres." He raises his eyes shyly to mine. "I hope this doesn't sound strange, but I've never dated one. We aren't very common, and I've always been attracted to, well..." He's sweating now, and he wipes it away with the back of his hand. "Something else, I suppose? I was in a relationship with a bigfoot for a while. After her, I dated a nymph, but that didn't go very far."

So he's been with others like me? Nymphs are a little taller than humans, but similar in shape and size. They're just lucky they have forest magic to protect them out in the world, or else they might be monster meat, too.

"Oh." So it's not that he's attracted to humans, specifically, he's just really not into his own kind. "Okay. That makes sense."

"That was probably a lot of information you didn't need to know," Egorr says with a self-deprecating chuckle.

"No!" I say it a little too loud. "I mean, no, it's helpful for me. And I sort of understand." Should I fess up? The fact I've also tried to date and failed? "Part of the reason I didn't call sooner, Egorr... is I got out of a relationship that went wrong."

Egorr's whole face falls. His big, bulky jaw is overtaken by his frown. "I'm so sorry."

I shrug, pretending to be much more aloof than I feel. "It's okay. We weren't a good fit. I think he was using me so he wouldn't feel lonely." I swallow hard to keep the pain and betrayal from showing on my face. "Just took me a while to get over it."

"But you were clearly still sad when it ended," Egorr says, reaching across the space between the couches to put a big, comforting hand on my arm. It's gigantic, each of his blunt fingernails twice as big as my own thumb.

"Yeah," I admit. "I guess I was sad. I thought it was for real between us, and it wasn't. He made that pretty clear by the end."

He nods. "I felt that way about Asha. My last girlfriend." He sighs. "But it was completely one-sided. We went on a few dates, and I fell hard for her, but she wasn't interested, not really. She cheated on me only a few months into the relationship."

Instantly, I'm incensed. She *cheated* on him?

"Wow, what a bitch," I say, without thinking twice about it. Then I cover my mouth. "Oh my gosh, I'm sorry. I don't know her at all. I shouldn't have said that."

Egorr's laugh is big and booming, and his grin is affectionate.

"You're fiery, Maddie," he says, his nose twitching. "I like it."

Now I'm the one taken aback that such a chill, quiet guy wouldn't mind me being a bit of a brat. "You do?"

The big ogre sits forward on his couch, closer to me, like he wants to say something private. I can't help but lean forward, too, so he can whisper to me whatever it is he wants to say.

"And that guy of yours?" he rumbles in my ear. "He's a bastard."

I don't try to hold in my giggle. Egorr pulls away, both of us smiling. I decide then that I like him. He is handsome, in his

14

own unusual way. His grin is infectious, and so honest and genuine that I feel warm all over.

I feel like I can trust Egorr.

"Thanks," I say with a breath of relief. "Honestly, he was an asshole." But now I have a chance for something different.

This time, I'm the one who puts a hand on Egorr's knee. He arches an eyebrow.

"Egorr?" I ask.

"Yes?" He puts his hand on top of mine, and a shiver runs up my arm. We've only just met, but already we're holding hands. And damn, I like it.

"Do you want to go on a date?" I ask. "Wherever you want. I don't care."

He's surprised at first, but his expression quickly shifts to pleased. "I would really love that, Maddie." He squeezes my hand a little tighter. "But you should pick the place, since you're the one who lives in here and doesn't get to go out much."

I think about that. If I could go anywhere, where would I go? Besides the Bahamas, of course.

"How about an amusement park?" I ask, already feeling giddy. "I've always wanted to ride a rollercoaster!"

Egorr lets out another wonderful laugh. "Okay. I've only been on one in my life before, but I'd be happy to go ride a rollercoaster with you."

Something about the way he says *with you* makes me feel warm and fluffy all over. I think he likes me, and boy, does that feel good.

We make plans to meet over the weekend, when Egorr is available, and run them by Samantha. Then the date is set.

When Egorr leaves, I wave goodbye, and his shy wave back makes my heart melt. Saturday can't possibly get here fast enough.

Chapter Three

J'm bouncing on my toes for the rest of the week, eagerly anticipating my date with Egorr. Celeste is a little smug when I tell her how our meeting went and that we hit it off.

"Hmm," she says, dealing the cards, "he sounds like a good guy."

"I think he is." Of course, I won't truly know for a while yet. People don't always show their true colors at first, or so I learned with Shisek. "At the very least, he seems genuine." And that goes a long way with me.

Then, finally, it's Saturday morning, and I wait with one of the guards outside the walls of New Eden for Egorr to pick me up. He arrives a few minutes early, to my great satisfaction, in a tiny green sedan. When he gets out of it, I hold back the temptation to hug him. I think it would feel good to hug someone as big and soft-looking as Egorr.

We both stand there for a moment facing each other, not sure if we should shake hands, hug, or do nothing. Egorr chuckles and rubs the back of his bare head.

"Should we go before it gets too busy?" he asks, and I hastily nod.

"Yeah, absolutely." I make my way to the passenger side of the car and slide inside. Egorr has to crouch down low to fit back into the driver's seat, and even then, he looks like a bear squashed inside a box. He starts the car up and pulls away from New Eden.

"Um..." I puzzle at how he's hunched over the steering wheel. "Why do you have such a small car?" I know it's rude, but I'm not sure how else to ask.

"It was cheap, and it's fuel efficient," Egorr says, shifting into fifth gear as we get onto the highway. "Plus, it never has mechanical problems. They don't make cars like this anymore."

He must make decent money as a software developer, but something about this big ogre fitting into a tiny little vehicle is immensely charming. It's plenty spacious for me, so I'm not complaining.

We chat about Egorr's last experience at an amusement park when he was just a teenager, and one of his classmates puked all over him on the pirate ship ride. It's horrifying and gross and so funny that I'm cackling and Egorr is snorting by the time he pulls into the parking lot.

I've never been to an amusement park before, of course, and I didn't realize just how *loud* it would be. There are monsters everywhere, adults and children alike swarming the entrance. I know I should stay close to Egorr, in case some passing creature thinks I'm there without a chaperone, but it's hard to keep up when I'm amazed by the bustle of activity. Near the ticket booth, we stand in line behind a cyclops mother trying to wrestle her little one-eyed children into line, and they squawk and holler like seagulls.

"Two, please," Egorr says when we get up to the counter, and pays for our tickets. Then we're inside.

"Wow," I say, gazing upward as one of the rollercoaster trains goes right over our heads. Monsters of all sorts scream as it rockets skyward. "That's really cool. And scary. But also cool."

"Do you want to get a snack first, or hop right on?" Egorr asks, strolling next to me with his hands in his pockets. He's wearing a casual navy T-shirt today, and a pair of nice jeans over his big frame. I wanted to impress him, so I wore a little yellow dress with comfortable shoes. Now that I've seen the rollercoaster go upside down, though, I'm seriously regretting my choice to not wear pants.

"Snack sounds good," I say. "I've always heard they have good food at these things."

"I wouldn't call it 'good,' per se." Egorr snickers. "But deep fried, delicious, and probably not very good for your intestinal tract? Absolutely."

I crack up. Something about his sense of humor makes me feel so at home, like I could say whatever stupid joke pops into my head and he'd probably like it.

We get one big funnel cake each, but I can only eat a third of mine. When he's done with his, Egorr chomps down the rest of it.

"Oh yeah, the meal thing," I say as we walk around the park, a few little wolf-children running past us. "I eat three times a day, you know."

He nods. "That's what the packet told me. No problem. The more I can eat, the better." He slaps his big belly, and I grin. He's so comfortable in his own skin, and it makes me feel more at ease in mine, too.

"Great." I pat my own belly. "You'd better get used to it, because I like to eat."

Egorr arches an eyebrow at me as he smiles, but doesn't say anything. I suppose I did make a rather bold assumption that we'd see each other again after this, but I have a hard time imagining what Egorr could do that would turn me off.

Hopefully he feels the same way.

I sidle closer to him as we pass a group of teenage monsters —a gorgon, an orc, and what appears to be some kind of ghoul— but none of them pay me any heed at all, too absorbed in their own conversation. So far, very few monsters seem to have noticed me, and those who do stare for a few moments before going back to whatever they were doing before.

Maybe all the warnings we were given about the outside world were just scaremongering.

"Hey." I tug on Egorr's sleeve. "Why don't we get on a ride now?"

His face lights up. "Sounds like a plan. Let's go."

The first rollercoaster we choose is meant for children, which seems like a good place to start. Some kids groan when they get in and find themselves sitting behind the massive Egorr. I tuck my dress under my legs and hold onto the bars as the rollercoaster starts moving. Slowly, the cars inch up and up a rather high peak.

"Is this the ride?" I whisper to Egorr. "Kind of boring."

He snorts. "Just wait." He offers me his hand. "Hold onto me if you need it."

"Why would I need it?" I ask, just as we reach the very top... and the rollercoaster dives downward.

Now I understand why everyone was screaming. The ground is rushing up toward me, so I seize Egorr's huge hand in mine, only managing to wrap my fingers around his big thumb as we fall to the earth. I holler my head off the whole way.

Then we reach the bottom of the track and swing back up again. We're moving even faster now, rocketing toward the next curve, and I'm holding onto Egorr's hand even tighter than before. He bellows with laughter next to me as we loop around and then dive again. I'm glad he's having a good time because I can't decide if I'm thrilled or terrified. Maybe a little of both.

It's intoxicating.

When we get off the ride, my legs are wobbly and my head is swimming. Egorr holds me upright, letting me lean against his much bigger body, until I finally have my wits about me again.

"Wow," I say, staring up at the tracks as the train goes by with a fresh batch of victims on board. "That was fucking awesome."

Egorr laughs again, and I'd be lying if I said I didn't love it. Making him laugh is easy, and I like how he doesn't seem to care who hears him.

"Then why don't we do another one?" he says. "We have all day."

On instinct, I grab his hand in mine again, and he squeezes back.

"Yeah! I'd love that."

We get on ride after ride, though there's only one where I'm denied entry for not being tall enough. We barter and beg with the ride operator, but he's insistent on the rules, even as he gives me a wide-eyed look.

"Haven't seen a human before," he says, cocking a brow. "But sorry. It's too dangerous for you."

With a sigh, we move on to the massive tower where people are buckled in and then sent plummeting to the earth.

"This looks terrifying," I say with a grin. "Can we do it?"

Egorr nods gamely. "Of course."

The rest of the day speeds by. After riding half a dozen rides, we eat some corndogs, and I have one while Egorr has four. We only get to ride a few more rides before, with a sigh, Egorr announces that he should probably take me home.

I barely register the drive back to the preserve that evening because we're so lost in conversation.

"So basically, your job is to find mistakes other people made and fix them?" I ask.

Egorr nods as we pull up to the front gates of New Eden. "Yup. Usually, all you have to do is walk backwards from what they were trying to accomplish, and then suss out what common mistakes they might have made along the way."

"Huh. That must mean you know how to do their jobs pretty well."

He shrugs shyly. "I guess. I was a programmer for a long time, but bug-hunting is more fun. It's creative, trying to figure out where it's coming from and then how to crush it."

I like how passionate Egorr is about his job, and I think I understand better now why he stays late at work. It's his hobby, too.

As we pull up outside New Eden, though, all my good humor drains away. I had such an amazing time out in the world, at Egorr's side, that I don't want it to end. Our adventure wasn't nearly as frightening as I expected—just the opposite. I felt safe and at home with him, even surrounded by an amusement park full of monsters.

I've been told all my life I should be afraid, that all it takes is one lone vampire to end you, but I felt nothing like that today.

"Hey," Egorr says as he puts the car in park. He turns to me and places his hand over mine on the console. "It was so much fun getting to know you more. I had an amazing time."

My heart beats faster. Is he going to ask me on another date? Is he going to *kiss* me?

"I did, too." I turn my hand over so our palms are touching. "Like, a really good time."

Egorr is a little quiet, but it's simply that he doesn't talk to fill space. He loves conversation, and especially if it leads to a good laugh.

I lean forward, absorbing the sight of his unusual face, which is hot in its own way. I like how big and sturdy his body is, and how easy it was today to be with him.

Fuck, I hope he'll kiss me.

Egorr takes in my expression, and a sideways smile pulls at his cheek. He leans closer to me, too.

"I've wanted to kiss you all day," he says, his breath tickling my nose. It smells like funnel cake.

"Is that right?" I inch a little closer until our noses are almost touching. "Why didn't you?"

"I wanted to give you space, for a first date." His smile widens. "And I wanted to find out if you were interested, too."

"Oh," I say, lowering my eyelashes. "I'm interested."

Almost before I can finish my sentence, Egorr is kissing me. Luckily, my small face fits neatly between his two big tusks, so our lips easily meet. His are much larger and thicker than mine, but once we figure out how we fit together... oh, wow.

First, he's much gentler than I expected from someone his size. Egorr sucks my lower lip in between his, lightly caressing it with his tongue before releasing it, then repeating that same delicious tactic on my upper lip. He's not forceful, but his kiss is still firm, still delectable. If I had any doubt that he liked me, the ferocity of this kiss wipes that doubt off the face of the planet.

I slide my hand up Egorr's arm to his cheek, and then over one of his tusks. I hold on to it as he kisses me deeper, his big arm curling around my back so he can apply even more pressure without pushing me out of my seat.

And then his tongue comes out to play. Oh, does it set me on fire when he licks the seam of my lips like that, and most happily, I open for him. The moment we meet in the middle, it's like that fire has taken to a field of dry grass, and it spreads all across my body. Now Egorr's hand has crawled up my back until he's holding the back of my head, and I'm sliding across the seat toward the console, my seatbelt digging uncomfortably into my hip. I don't care for even a second, though, as Egorr's mouth simply crushes mine, and his tongue plays me like I'm a piano and he's Mozart.

Damn. I bet he's really good in bed.

When we finally pull away from our kiss, I'm panting from not having enough oxygen. Egorr chuckles, letting go of my body but not releasing my hand.

"So do you want to go out again?" he asks, a little self-satisfied smirk on his face. I like when he's cheeky.

"Um." I have to get my thoughts in order, and his smile falls. "I was thinking, actually..."

"It's okay if you don't. I won't pressure you."

"No, no." I cradle his hand against my chest. "What I wanted to say was—maybe we should go to the next level, instead?"

"The next level?" he asks, brow furrowing. "I don't think they let monsters onto the compound, and my house is a ways away—"

"Not that, silly. Well, not right now, anyway." I waggle my eyebrows, and Egorr's lips part in surprise. "I mean, do you want to just do it? The trial marriage?"

Maybe it's crazy after being dumped by Shisek. Maybe I'm using Egorr as a rebound, and that's why I'm moving so quickly. Maybe I'm the kind of person who can't stand being alone, and what if I'm just using him?

But it's not any of that. No, I have a good feeling about

Egorr. A *great* feeling. I think we could have something really special, and I don't want to waste time going on more dates when I already know what I want, and that's to find out if we're truly compatible.

"Really?" Egorr asks, dumbfounded. I slide my hands down his arms.

"Yeah. If you want to." I lean back a little. "I don't want to pressure you, either."

Vigorously, Egorr shakes his head. "I'm just surprised. In a good way."

He leans down and kisses me again, and I find myself sliding farther over the console toward him. This kiss is even more intense than the first one, and it's sending little waves of warmth all over my body.

"Wait, one second," Egorr says, panting as he pulls away from our kiss. Then he grabs the handle under his seat and pushes it back, leaving a big space between his belly and the steering wheel. He unclips my seatbelt, reaches around my waist, and pulls me by the hips into his lap.

I squeak as I settle there, my ass right over his crotch, my legs bent against the seat. Egorr's huge hands caress me as he looks into my eyes.

"I would love that," Egorr says in an even lower voice than before. "To have you in my home? I can't imagine anything better." That's when I feel it—something rather bulky poking at the underside of my thighs. "I'll need a few days to get things ready, but..."

"Of course," I say, maybe too eagerly, but it just makes Egorr smile.

"It's not too soon for you?" He tilts his head down. "I know you just had your heart broken."

"Only if it's not too soon for you," I say, stroking one of his tusks. "I'm over that asshole Shisek."

Egorr grins as he leans forward and circles me with his arms, then crushes me in a hug. He brings his lips to my ear.

"Not at all." His breaths are growing faster. "I would love to share my home with you."

The way he says it, like it would be a one-way bus ticket, makes my heart race with glee.

"Good." I can't help rubbing my ass over that lump in his pants, and he lets out a groan. "Get your ducks in a row and come back for me when you're ready, then?"

With that, I open the car door and slide out, leaving Egorr dazed. I give him a kiss on the cheek before heading inside, where I'll once more be locked behind the high walls of the preserve.

But at least now, I know my path out, and it's at the side of a big, green ogre.

Chapter Four

I'm absolutely buzzing with excitement—and a tad of horniness—by the time I get back to my house. The second I'm in the door, I call Celeste to tell her what happened.

I did it. I asked Egorr to take the next step with me, and he agreed. I'm simply soaring.

"You're doing a trial marriage already?" Celeste asks the second she arrives at my house. Her lips screw up in uncertainty. "But you just spent the last month getting over Shisek, Maddie. Are you sure it's wise to jump in so soon with someone else?"

"I know, I know." I put on some hot water while we talk. "But I have a good feeling about him. A *really* good feeling. We got along great, we had an amazing time together, and we have serious chemistry. I just want to know if it'll work out or not before I invest too much more in him."

"A trial marriage is a big investment," Celeste says in that even tone that says she's trying to bring me back down to earth. Then she narrows her eyes at me. "You want to sleep with him, don't you?"

My shoulders curl defensively. Sitting on Egorr's lap certainly didn't do anything to remove that possibility from my mind.

"Is it so bad that it's important to me?"

Celeste sighs. "I guess not. I just don't want you to rush into anything and then maybe..."

"What, ruin it?" I ask. My tone is more biting than I mean it to be, but I still feel responsible for what happened with Shisek. I still wonder, even now, if I was the issue, if I was the reason it all fell apart.

"No," Celeste says, with a pitying look. "I just don't want to see you get hurt again."

If I know anything, though, it's that Egorr won't hurt me. He would never. He's a gentle giant with a funny, playful side. He's sweet and thoughtful, and even a little dirty. He has a good heart.

I wave her off. "It'll be fine. I know what I'm getting into this time. I've done a trial marriage before." I don't mean it as a jab, since Celeste has never gone on more than one or two dates with a monster, but I can tell by the look in her eyes that she's hurt.

"You'll find someone to go home with, too," I say quickly, apologetically. "I know you will."

"Maybe." Celeste gets up to make the tea now that I've forgotten all about the kettle. "So tell me about your date with Egorr. What made you so sure?"

"Well," I begin, "He had the biggest boner I've ever felt in my life."

She bursts out laughing.

"Kidding," I say. I have to think a little harder about an honest answer. "I think it was that I could be myself, you know? I didn't have to be quieter or change my sense of humor. He just... accepted me. He thought my jokes were funny. And he held my hand. A lot."

Celeste quirks an eyebrow. "That's what does it for you, huh?"

"Shush. But it was a nice touch."

"I'm sure he'll have lots of other nice touches for you, too," she says, and I can't help cackling.

I hope so. I really hope so.

Telling my parents about my decision is much easier than telling Celeste. I fill them in on our first date—minus the part where I sat on Egorr's lap and we made out—and they're thrilled for me.

"I think someone like this would be a good fit for you," Mom says, reaching around my shoulders to squeeze me in a hug. "Much more genuine than that *Shisek.*" She practically spits the name, and I have to laugh.

At the end of the week, after Egorr has had some time to prepare his home for me, it's time to go. It's a Saturday, so we'll have all weekend to get me settled before Egorr has to go back to work. In my little house on the preserve, I pack up what I think I'll need, hoping that I won't have to bring it back.

Mom and Dad wait with me at the entrance to New Eden for Egorr to arrive. He's right on time, pulling up in his tiny sedan and popping the trunk open. I run out into the road to hug him, ready to be wrapped up in his soft arms again, and he chuckles as he brings me in close. He kisses the top of my head.

"Are you ready?" he asks, just for my ears. "To start the rest of your life?"

I shiver all over at how enticing that sounds. I'm definitely ready for my happily ever after with Egorr.

"You sure know what to say to a girl," I say, standing up on my tiptoes to kiss his lips.

"What about us?" Mom grouses, and I apologize before introducing them to Egorr. He shakes Dad's hand firmly, and even my father is thrown by how big he is.

"Good handshake," Dad mutters, rubbing his hand afterwards.

After we've signed off on all the paperwork, my parents help load my bags into the back seat and the trunk of Egorr's car. Egorr quirks an eyebrow when he sees the pile of three suitcases and two duffel bags, but doesn't complain.

I hug my parents goodbye, and then it's time to go. But before I can get inside the car, Egorr stops me. He has to bend down quite a ways for his mouth to get anywhere near mine.

"Your room is all set up at home," he says in a seductive voice. "And I have some presents, too."

"Presents?" I immediately brighten. "For me?"

He pauses with his lips just brushing mine. "For you."

Then he kisses me, hard, and I drown in him. Damn. Who knew ogres could kiss like champs? He picks me up by the waist and swings me around while he devours me, and I feel like I'm flying. I hope my landing will be soft this time.

"Save it for later!" Mom calls out, and I blush as we get into the car. And then, at last, we're on our way.

Egorr lives on the edge of town to the east. I remember what the Wikipedia article said about ogres living in hills and mountains, and sure enough, soon we start to head upward. We've been winding around twisting roads and through hilly countryside for a few minutes when Egorr takes a left turn down a cute little street, with houses that aren't too close together. He stops in front of a massive oak tree and takes a quick right before pulling into a driveway.

There in front of us is... well, a door. A big wooden door,

built right into the side of the hill, with a gorgeous stained glass window in the middle. We hop out of the car, and Egorr leads me by the hand to the house buried in a hillside.

"Here we are." He turns the knob and pulls the door open. "Home sweet home."

Inside it's dark at first, until Egorr reaches in and flips a switch, bathing everything in soft light.

It's homey inside. That's the best way I can describe this warm, cozy place. The walls and ceiling are dome-shaped, and a little skylight peers down from above. There's a fireplace with a couch in front of it, and a well-loved chair by a television. A tidy kitchen with a big island is tucked into the back corner of the open floor plan, and next to it are a small table and two chairs. One of them is very big, and one of them...

"This is the first present," Egorr says, eagerly walking over to the much smaller chair that looks brand new. He picks it up and shows it to me, hefting its whole weight like it's a matchstick. "I thought you'd be more comfortable with this than with one of my big chairs."

It's so thoughtful, I can't speak for a moment.

Egorr tilts his head, concern furrowing his brow. "Maddie?"

"Ohmygosh." It all spills out at once. I throw my arms around him, and he laughs as he hugs me back. "It's really cute. And wonderful. And thoughtful. Thank you."

He nods, his green cheeks turning a darker shade of olive, then he takes me by the hand and leads me down the hall.

"This is my room," he says, nodding at an open doorway. I peer inside, but it's too dark to make anything out. "And this is your room." He turns the knob on the next door and pushes it wide open for me.

Inside there's light—lots of it—coming in through a deep window that burrows out of the hill. The room is small and round, like the rest of the house, with a twin bed on an antique bronze frame.

"I went around to the thrift stores to find things that might match," he says sheepishly. "I didn't want to get you some cheap Ikea stuff."

"Wow." I run my hand over the comforter, then the worn wood bedside table that has a little lamp shaped like a tulip. "It's so cute." There are butterflies doing somersaults in my stomach just seeing how much thought he put into this room. He really wanted to make sure I'd be comfortable here.

"You think so?" Egorr grins at me. "Good. I didn't know what your taste would be, so feel free to redecorate it how you please." He demonstrates how to close the big heavy curtains. "If you want to sleep in, you can close these."

Part of me hopes I won't be sleeping here much, but I don't want to dive into things too quickly, either. I wonder if Egorr's ever lived with a partner before, but it didn't sound like any of his relationships had gotten serious enough for that.

He shows me to the small bathroom we'll share, then brings in my bags so I can get unpacked. With a peck on my cheek, he leaves me to it while he makes lunch.

I hang up each of my outfits in the closet, and I think I like the look of them here.

That afternoon, we decide to go out to the store together to buy things I might want to have around the house while Egorr's at work. He pushes the rather large cart, and I dart up and down the aisles, finding all sorts of snacks I've never even seen before.

"Egorr!" I say, bounding over with a box of sandwich cookies. "These have lemon filling. Can you believe that?"

He chuckles. "You want them?"

"Um, yes!" My mouth is watering just looking at the big illustration on the box.

"Then add them to the cart." Even the frozen food aisle is incredible to me. It's like they have every option on the planet and then some.

"What did you eat at New Eden?" Egorr asks as I grab a box of frozen jalapeño poppers and add it to the growing pile in the cart.

"Oh, you know. Mashed potatoes and gravy. Salad. Pizza, sometimes." In the cafeteria, we usually had three options for each meal. Here... the options are limitless. Speaking of which, we've just stopped in the frozen food aisle, in front of a huge freezer completely full of pizza.

"Holy shit." I can hear angels singing. "This is incredible."

"You know, delivery is probably better—" Egorr begins, but I'm already choosing the best-looking pepperoni pizza they have. He doesn't object when I add it to the pile.

"Wow." I gaze down row after row of food options. "The grocery store is amazing." And I get to choose from all of it.

"Ready to check out?" Egorr asks when we've explored all the way from one end of the store to the other. I'm breathless.

"Yes. Yes, I think so." I turn to him. "We're definitely coming back here."

Egorr gets a big grin on his face. "We can come to the store whenever you want."

We get in line at check-out behind what appears to be nothing but a skeleton dressed in a long, black cloak. It turns around briefly to look at us, and the bare holes in its skull make me squeak in alarm. I reflexively grab Egorr's arm, and I can't tell what the skeleton is thinking because, well, it doesn't have a face. It turns away and starts loading goods onto the conveyor belt, shaking its head.

"Sorry," I say to Egorr, letting go of him. He tilts his head down.

"This must all be pretty new for you, huh?" The skeleton steps forward to check out, and Egorr puts a divider on the conveyor belt between our groceries and theirs. "I can't imagine what it's like living on the preserve your whole life."

"I've definitely never seen that before," I say quietly, gesturing at the skeleton. I wonder if skeletons ever apply for human companions. It might be hard without lips. Or... you know.

"You said you did another trial marriage, right?" Egorr asks. He rests a hand on my lower back. "The one that didn't work out. Did you never go to the grocery store?"

I swallow. "Yeah. Though he didn't eat anything at all, and he just brought home the bare minimum. We didn't even go to a restaurant once."

"Well, we can go out all you want." Egorr puts yet another box of cookies on the conveyor belt. "Or stay in, if that's your thing."

"I'm not sure what my 'thing' is, to be honest," I say, helping with the fruit and vegetables.

"I guess we'll find out then, won't we?"

Egorr grins. Am I imagining the slightly filthy lilt to his voice when he says it?

Once the cart is empty, he talks to the cashier—a basilisk in a pair of sunglasses, her tail curled up around her to fit into the checkout stand. She rings everything up, filling all the bags Egorr brought along and a few extras because we bought so many things.

Oops.

Then we've loaded it all in the car and we're heading home.

"I liked that," I say. "Maybe my 'thing' is going to the grocery store."

Egorr's laugh fills up the whole car.

Chapter Five

Though we just bought a ton of groceries, all I can think about is the delivery pizza Egorr mentioned at the store. I've always seen it on TV, showing up at someone's house warm and steaming and melty, and I'm curious what it's like to get my food delivered.

When I tell him what I want, Egorr doesn't question my choice and quickly calls in one cheese pizza, one pepperoni pizza, and wings on the side. It's a ton of food, but I have no doubt that someone Egorr's size can eat it all.

When our food arrives, still steaming hot, it's absolutely heavenly. I've never had anything like delivery pizza in my life.

"It's even better than it looks on TV," I tell Egorr, thinking of all the ads I watched back at New Eden. "Like, this is unbelievable."

"If only I'd known all it took to woo a girl was to get her some pizza." Egorr winks.

I think he's coming on to me, and I'm all about it.

"Consider me wooed," I say, shimmying my chair a little closer to his. I'm just about done eating anyway, even though there's more than half a pie left. But Egorr makes quick work of it, and when he's finished, he lets out a satisfied groan.

I'm in the same boat. I probably couldn't move a muscle after everything I just ate.

Eventually we migrate to the couch, where we sit side by side as we talk. I've always been chatty, or so my mother tells me, but Egorr doesn't seem to mind at all. He spends a lot of time listening, like when I go on about my friends and family, simply stroking the back of my hand.

"What about you?" I finally ask, realizing I've been dominating the conversation. "Where's your family?"

He strokes his chin. "Well, my parents aren't together anymore. I don't speak to my mom often, though, because she married a weird guy who doesn't like me very much."

I gape at him. "But you're her son!"

Egorr just smiles. "It's okay. My dad and I are really close. He lives about forty-five minutes away. Never got remarried, but I think he's happier like that."

"That's not far. We should visit him!"

That smile widens even more, and I love the way Egorr's grin reveals all of his teeth, top and bottom rows alike.

"Sure. He's a quiet guy, but I think you two would get along."

He sounds as if he might be a lot like his son.

I don't even realize I've started falling asleep on Egorr's shoulder until my head lands on something soft, and I jerk awake.

"Ready for bed?" Egorr hums in my ear. It sounds so sexy when he says it like that, but I know he means my own bed in the room he set up for me. We're not there yet, but I hope we are soon.

"Yeah, I guess," I say with a yawn. But before I can get up, Egorr slides an arm under my back and another under my legs, hefting me up into his arms like I'm little more than a doll. I giggle as he carries me down the hall to my room, and pushes the door open with his shoulder.

There, he lays me down on my bed ever so gently. I feel airy and weightless from being carried, and I'm warm and fuzzy after devouring amazing pizza—not to mention how at home I already feel here in this big ogre's den.

"Egorr," I say quietly when he starts to pull away. He stops, remaining crouched over me as I lift a hand up to his tusk and wrap my fingers around it. I tug his face toward mine, and with a smile, Egorr leans down closer, until our lips are almost touching.

"Maddie," he says in return, making me giggle. I lift my head between his tusks and push my lips up against his.

Egorr returns it, sliding one arm under my back to bring us closer together. Boy, is he a good kisser. I sink into it, giving him everything. Our tongues both dart out to dance, and I sure do love how big his is, dwarfing mine as they play together. His wide hands are eager but not forceful, gentle but not delicate.

Eventually, we both pull away, breathing hard.

Egorr kisses me on the forehead. "Get some sleep," he says, rising back up to his full height. "We have another day of fun tomorrow, and I want to get a head start."

"Okay." I fall back to the bed. "Goodnight."

"Goodnight, Maddie."

Egorr closes the door behind him, and though I'm sad to see him go, I'm excited to sleep in this sweet little room he prepared for me. I love the antique bed frame, the worn wooden side table, and the cute, kitschy lamp that looks like it belongs in a grandmother's house.

Besides, I think it might be wise of me to maintain my own space while I try to integrate into Egorr's life—to have a separation between what's his and what's mine in case we decide to part ways later on.

Just the thought of it makes my heart hurt, though. I've already grown so attached to him.

It might be a tad presumptuous of me to think I'll fit into Egorr's world, or that I'll be sticking around long enough for it to matter. Maybe things look rosy now, but you never know when a monster like Shisek might decide you're too much trouble and send you packing.

I have to hope that won't be Egorr.

The next morning, I wake up late. The smell of cooking bacon draws me out of my room, and I'm glad it's Sunday so Egorr doesn't have to go to work. I want to get to know him better, what makes him tick, and see if he could really be the one for me.

"Maddie!" Egorr's eyes light up when he sees me, and mine probably do, too, when I walk in on him bustling about the kitchen. The fire is going in the fireplace, which means it's probably quite cold outside, and the open living room has a cozy feel about it. I spend more time than I should just staring at him and his enormous body, taking in his bulging pectorals and the swell of his belly. He's wearing yet another pair of casual sweatpants, and I like that he's not putting on any airs for me. This is probably how he spent his time before I came here, just busying about in nothing but sweats, and I like knowing what my life could look like in the future with Egorr.

"Good morning," I say, strolling into the kitchen. He leans down to kiss my forehead, and in return, I rise up onto my tiptoes to kiss him on the cheek. I'm rewarded with a chuckle.

"I hope you wanted bacon and eggs, because that's about as

far as my breakfast repertoire goes." He pulls a pan off the stove and uses a pair of tongs to pull out steaming-hot strips of bacon, dropping them onto a pair of plates waiting on the island. Then follow the eggs, scrambled with herbs and served alongside ketchup.

I sit on one of the stools at the island while Egorr pours out grapefruit juice for both of us, then joins me. We eat in companionable silence until we've both cleared off our plates.

"What would you like to do today?" Egorr asks as he takes them away and tucks them into the dishwasher.

I haven't even thought about it. For some reason, I pictured him with plans already that I would simply have to fit into.

"How much time do we have?" I ask, wondering which activities we can fit in when he's free. I have a laundry list of things I'd like to do in the world, but Egorr has a life already, and I don't want to intrude too much.

But he just blinks at me. "Well, we have all day, if you want. You're my priority."

He's giving me his whole Sunday? Damn it, I could just hug him.

So I do. I can't help but throw myself at him, wrapping my arms as far as I can around his bulk. Egorr pats my head.

"I have too many ideas," I say, finally pulling away.

"Well, tell me the first few."

I put up one finger. "I really want to try rock climbing." I put up a second finger. "And zip lining." Then a third finger. "I've always thought about learning to fence." A fourth finger. "Forging? I used to watch this TV show about forging and it looked like so much fun." Before I can add a fifth finger, Egorr is laughing, and he covers my hand with his.

"Okay, we can probably fit in one of those today," he says. "I think you have to make reservations for a zip line." He tilts his head. "Forging? Like what?"

"Knives, of course!"

My enthusiasm is met with an arched eyebrow. "What would you use said knife for?"

That seems like a silly question. "Well, to cut stuff." I rub my chin. "It would probably also look good on my wall."

"Do you want to decorate?" he asks. "I didn't put up any pictures in your room in case you wanted to choose them for yourself."

"Yes! As long as it's with a knife I made. I think that would be cool."

Egorr pulls out his phone and starts Google searching. "There is a local forge where you can sign up for classes," he says. "Why don't we do that? It would be a weekly thing, though, and we couldn't get into a class until next week."

I like the idea of making plans that far in advance. I hope I'm still here in a week, enjoying Egorr and his cozy home.

"Then we'd better find something to do in the meantime," I say brightly.

Egorr grins in return. "There's a rock climbing gym nearby. It's a walk-in type of place. I've never done it, but we could go check it out if you want."

"Sounds good. I'd love to."

When we pull up to the rock climbing gym, there are all sorts of monsters heading inside dressed in their workout clothes. As we get out of the car, Egorr takes my hand, and I like how familiar it feels already to have my fingers swallowed up by his palm.

We each rent a pair of climbing shoes. Unfortunately, I'm much smaller than most monsters, so my shoes are a little too big. Egorr assures me we're starting with the easiest climbs, so it shouldn't be a problem.

At the beginner wall, the routes are marked with tape and numbered.

"You should do the zero routes first," the attendant tells us. I stare up at the high wall, suddenly wondering if I've made a mistake in my choice of activity. It looks scary up there. But plenty of other monsters are doing the climbs without a problem, so I square my shoulders and decide I'll give it a try.

When the bigfoot doing the zero-level route comes back down again, Egorr nods at me to give it a shot. I wrap my hand around the first hold, then grab the second one with my other hand, hefting myself up onto the footholds. Egorr stands below me, arms held out.

"If you find yourself falling," the attendant calls up to me, "be sure to twist your body so you don't land on your back."

That sounds like a mighty big ask, given I'll be in the middle of falling, but I nod anyway as I continue to the next pair of holds.

Wow. This uses a lot more upper-body strength than I expected. I navigate my feet up, holding on tight as I try to find the next set of holds with my toes. Still, it's not too hard. I get two-thirds of the way up the wall when I make the mistake of looking down.

"Oh shit," I mutter, realizing Egorr is much smaller down there than he should be. I take a few deep breaths, trying to still my heart. I'm really high up. If I fell right now...

"It's okay if you want to come back down," Egorr says, as if he can read my mind. Nodding quickly, I make my way to the previous set of holds, and I'm surprised at how much harder it is going back down than it was going up. I'm not sure where to put my feet.

"Egorr!" I can hear the fear in my own voice. "I can't get down."

"I'm here," he calls back. "If you jump down, I'll catch you."

Glancing down at him, with his big arms held out for me, I know he will. I exhale deeply and then hop off the wall.

Sure enough, he catches me. Gently, he lowers me to the ground, and I feel warm all over. I take a few deep breaths to calm my heart.

"Pretty high up there?" he asks, a comforting smile on his face.

"Yeah. I thought I was okay with heights, but..."

"You get used to it," the attendant says, a wolf-woman with rather long fangs. "It comes with practice."

That's comforting to hear.

It's Egorr's turn next, and he has a significantly harder time climbing the wall thanks to his bulk, but he's also incredibly strong and manages to make it a little farther up than I did. He's almost at the top when he freezes.

"Shit," I hear him mutter. "It *is* really high up here." Quickly he climbs down the wall again, and when he gets his feet back on the ground, he looks a tad shaken. I can't help but laugh.

"Maybe rock climbing isn't for us?" I say, rubbing his arm.

"Maybe not." He lets out a long breath. "I don't think ogres are meant for heights."

We try a few more short climbs, then decide we're not cut out for the rock climber life and turn in our shoes at the front desk. Egorr takes my hand again as we leave.

"That was fun, though," he says. "And now we know."

Chapter Six

*W*hen we get home from the gym, I'm exhausted and ready to plop down on the couch.

"I didn't think it would take quite so much out of me," I moan, rolling my shoulders. "Those muscles aren't going to feel the same again."

Egorr chuckles and takes my hand to lead me over to the fireplace. He sets me on the couch, then goes about lighting it before he joins me.

"Turn around?" he asks.

Curious, I do as he says, bringing my legs up into a crossed position and showing him my back. Egorr shifts behind me, then his huge hands land on my shoulders. The tips of his wide fingers press into my muscles, and it's the perfect combination of painful and heavenly.

"Ohhh." I instantly relax under him. "That's good."

Those big hands are surprisingly gentle but also precise as they work, testing out each muscle in my back and shoulders, then working the spots that are now cinched tight. When he finds a knot, he digs a little deeper, which is both wonderful and excruciating. I let out more whimpers and moans as he rubs his thumb over these tender places, and behind me, Egorr's breaths speed up. He leans down as he continues massaging me, bringing his lips close to my ear.

"I love the little noises you make," he murmurs, smoothing his hands over my shoulder blades. "It's so sexy."

I giggle, not realizing just how filthy I probably sounded. I lean back into Egorr's arms, and he curls them around me, bringing my head to rest under his chin.

"I can make lots more." I wiggle against him, and this time it's Egorr who lets out a sexy moan.

"I should cook us something," he says eventually, releasing me from his grip. "Refuel that tired little body of yours."

I'm sad when he gets up, but I quickly join him to try to make myself useful. He assigns me to chopping veggies while he prepares the meat, and soon delicious smells are filling up the whole house.

I could get used to home-cooked meals every night, that's for sure. When we dive in, we're silent until we've finished eating, both of us ravenous. When I'm finally done stuffing my face, I realize that it's Sunday night, and Egorr has to go back to work tomorrow.

"This was a really fun weekend," I say, reaching across the table to take his hand in mine. I can only get my fingers wrapped around his thumb, but he squeezes me back with a big grin on his wide face.

"Technically I have to work tomorrow, but I'm working from home," Egorr says. "My boss is giving me a little... flexibility."

I arch an eyebrow. "Oh? Because you just basically got married?"

His whole face darkens with embarrassment. "I have a big mouth and told all my coworkers when we went on a date. Now they all know that you're—"

"Human," I finish. He nods, rubbing his head. "Not a bad deal for me if I get to see you all day!"

He gives me a wide grin. "All day."

That night, before bed, Egorr pulls me into his arms and kisses me so fiercely that he lifts me off the ground. Even though I know it's a good idea to wait a little longer, I'm already so hungry for him that I wrap my legs around his waist and deepen the kiss. He grunts against me as he gets hard under his sweats, but eventually he does set me down again.

"Goodnight, little Maddie," he says, kissing my forehead before we part ways.

I wake up warm and cozy, a gentle sunbeam coming in the window through a gap in the curtains. I could definitely get used to this.

When I pull the curtains open, sun illuminates the whole little room. Since Egorr is working today, I'll have to finally finish unpacking, but I might need to ask him for another dresser to fit everything I brought along.

Once I'm dressed, I make my way out into the hallway, where I hear Egorr's voice.

"Can you send that file over to me, Bill? Yeah, I'll have time."

I step out into the living room to find Egorr perched at a desk in the corner of the living room in front of his computer. I duck when I realize the camera is pointed at me.

"It's okay," he calls over his shoulder. "You can come out,

Maddie." I step into the living room, and Egorr says, "Sorry, Bill. I'll talk to you later once I look things over." Then he shuts the computer and gets to his feet, dressed in a collared shirt and sweatpants. They cling to his hips, shamelessly showing off his rather large package. Egorr grins and stoops down, clearly waiting for a kiss.

Oh, and do I give him one. Our mouths collide in something much more exciting than a simple *good morning* kiss. His hands caress my hair, then slide down my neck to my back. I want him to keep going, so I lean my body into his, letting my boobs squish against his chest. My hips gently tease his, and Egorr's breath hitches. Those massive hands do finally explore lower, over the swell of my ass, and immediately his body responds.

"Maddie," he groans, pulling his mouth away from mine so he can look into my eyes. He smirks. "You know exactly what you do to me, don't you?"

I wiggle my lower body, brushing it over that slowly expanding lump in his sweatpants. Egorr's eyes close and he leans his forehead against mine, squeezing each of my ass cheeks.

"Maybe," I answer in a teasing voice.

"I have to work," Egorr says, despite his roaming fingers telling me he'd rather do anything but. He skates them back up my sides, pausing just inches away from touching my breasts. "But after that, I'm all yours."

A shudder passes through me. All mine, huh? I didn't realize how much I wanted to hear someone say that until Egorr did.

I release him, but then snatch one more small kiss from his lips before pulling away. Egorr rubs his bald head, and with his other hand, adjusts his sweatpants over the rather significant tent in the front. I love that he's hard for me. My pussy is practically aching now with how much I want to see it, and feel it, and...

"I love the work-from-home uniform," I tell him, gesturing at the combo of collared shirt and sweats.

Egorr grins. "The perks of a desk job. They only see me from the waist up." He heads to the kitchen, where he opens the fridge and pulls out a small pile of ingredients. "I was just about to make breakfast. Does bacon and eggs work for you again?"

"Oh yes," I say, hopping up on one of the bar stools. "Please."

He's quick about it, chopping things and throwing food into pans until it's all sizzling. Yep. I could definitely get used to this.

I'm accustomed to having very little to do after living on the preserve all my life, so it's no problem for me that Egorr has to work all day. I set right away to reading one of the books I grabbed off of his bookshelf, curling up on the couch with a blanket in front of the fireplace. The one I chose is an epic fantasy, with swords and dragons and big battles.

I chew an apple while Egorr takes another video call, talking with his coworkers about all sorts of computer-y things I don't understand, and for the first time in who knows how long, I feel... *happy*. I like listening to the sound of Egorr's deep voice and the tapping of his keyboard as he works. When the morning turns into afternoon, I start poking around the kitchen for the ingredients we bought, trying to think of what I could cook for us for dinner. I'm not the greatest cook ever, and I usually visited the cafeteria for my meals at New Eden, but I think I can put something together.

I look up a recipe online for stir fry and get started chopping vegetables.

I don't realize Egorr's gotten up from his desk until I feel big, soft hands on my shoulders. Egorr nuzzles his nose into my hair, and his big body gently presses against mine.

"I couldn't stop thinking about you today," he says, and his breathing is heavy. "It was torture not getting to kiss you more."

I giggle and lean toward him until my back is completely flush with his front. Egorr sucks in a breath.

"I know the feeling." I put the knife down, and he peers over my shoulder.

"Getting dinner ready?" he asks, kissing my neck. He pulls up my hair with one hand so he can continue dragging his lips across my nape.

"That was the plan," I say, shivering all over at the sensation of his mouth on me. "Until someone interrupted me."

He chuckles at my barb as he slides his hand down my front, stopping at my belly so he can press my hips back into his, wedging his cock between my ass cheeks.

Oh, fuck. My pussy tightens instantly.

"You really turn me on," Egorr whispers in my ear.

"You turn me on, too." I turn my head so I can kiss him on the cheek, and push my ass even more insistently at his groin. I'm not even hungry anymore for food—all I want is this gentle giant and whatever he's hiding under those sweatpants.

As if he can read my mind, Egorr slides away the knife and cutting board, then turns me around so we're facing one another. He seizes my lips in a kiss, and while we're enmeshed at the mouth, he wraps his hands around my thighs and hefts me up onto the counter. I squeak as he spreads my legs, hooking my thighs around his waist.

Now I can feel all of him, and his hidden gem is nudging eagerly between my legs through my leggings and underwear.

Oh, fuck. It's huge. Like... really, really huge. It's as if all my settings have been cranked up to ten because I'm wriggling against him without any conscious command, and Egorr lets out a huff in my ear.

"I've been fantasizing about touching you since I met you," he whispers in my ear.

"I hope you do a lot more than touch me."

Egorr's booming laugh makes me tingle. "If that's what you want."

His hands explore more freely, venturing between us to cup my breasts over my shirt. I lean into him, encouraging him. I'm tempted to just take my shirt off and let him have them. Then Egorr pauses, and I give him a questioning look.

"We probably should make dinner first," he says, his voice even lower and huskier. "But then..."

I pout. "I have to wait?"

He grins. "Just a little while. Then we can do whatever you want."

I light on fire at the thought of it. *Whatever I want?*

Oh, I'll have fun with that.

I finish with the vegetables while Egorr makes rice and pulls out chicken thighs. Cooking takes way too long, and by the time dinner is served, I'm bouncing on the balls of my feet for what we have planned next.

Egorr wants me. *Me.* And he's going to let me have my way with him.

Finally we're done eating, but before Egorr can clear away the plates, I grab his hand in mine and tug him toward the couch. He grins as I fall back on it, into the pillows, and I pull him down on top of me. He props himself up with one arm, letting the weight of his body press me into the cushions. I can't help a moan as his cock rests between my thighs.

"What do you want, little Maddie?" he asks, rocking his hips ever so slightly.

"Well, I want your dick, for starters," I say, and Egorr outright laughs. Is he making fun of me? Then he brings his head down to brush a kiss over my lips.

"Is that right?" he purrs. "And what will you do with it?"

"Probably suck on it." I drag my tongue across his mouth, and his whole body tenses above me. "And then…" I trail off, thinking of what else I'll do with that big cock once it's in my hands.

"And then?" he asks, shamelessly palming my breast through my shirt.

"And then I want it inside me."

Egorr groans, and his hips grind even more insistently against mine. "I have some things I want to do before that."

His wandering hand ducks under my shirt, venturing up to brush over my bra. My nipples are already hard as rocks underneath.

"What kinds of things?" I ask as he squeezes me, his hips dragging that tantalizing lump over my crotch again and again. "I'm not sure how long I can wait."

"I'll show you." Abruptly Egorr draws back, and I whimper as his mouth leaves mine. But he's not done with me. Kneeling between my legs, he pulls my shirt up, and I raise my arms so he can slip it the rest of the way over my head.

"Can you take this off?" he asks, hooking a finger under my bra. I nod hastily and reach behind my back to unhook it, and he pulls it off the same way. Then I'm topless in front of him, my tits out for the whole world to see.

"You're gorgeous," Egorr says with wonder in his voice. He takes one breast in his palm, rolling my nipple in his fingers, and I gasp at his warm touch. Then he drops his head and takes the other nipple in his mouth, sucking on it eagerly, flicking over it with his tongue while his long, cool tusks press into my chest. I already feel like I'm about to combust.

When he's finished sucking on my tits, Egorr raises his eyes to mine, and they're absolutely glittering with lust. Good. I turn him on just as much as he does me.

"Can we get naked?" I ask, lifting my hips to slide them over his groin again. "Please?"

Egorr's chuckle is warm and affectionate. "I'd love to."

Chapter Seven

*E*gorr gets up and sets me on the ground, where I hastily pull down my leggings. When I look up, his shirt is gone, and I'm mesmerized.

My ogre's chest is huge, with full pectorals and arms as thick as tree trunks. He has the body of a power lifter, with a hefty belly that promises to feel very good on top of me, and, potentially, below me. Egorr drags his sweatpants down with a thumb, along with his boxers.

My eyes must go wide as saucers when I see it. Holy shit. His cock is... amazing. It pops out, now free from its prison, thick and erect for me. It's green, like him, with a soft, round head eagerly poking out from under the foreskin.

And wow—while I expected something big, this is *big*. I wonder if he's considered well-hung for an ogre, or if that's just how they all are?

Without thinking, I reach out to touch it, all my instincts telling me to get my hands around it and guide it between my legs where it certainly belongs. Egorr lets out a halting breath when I circle him with my fingers and then squeeze.

"Oh, wow," I say with wonder, and he grins down at me.

"What do you think?"

I tighten my grasp, testing out every inch of this massive thing. I've had sex with people on the preserve before, but they were all human, and none of them compare to Egorr.

"It's incredible." I kneel so I can get closer to it, and lean forward to bring it into my mouth, but Egorr stops me.

"If you do that, I won't last."

I waggle my eyebrows. "Then don't last, and we can go again!"

But Egorr just shakes his head. "Not yet."

He leans down, sliding his hands under my arms to lift me into the air. Instinctively, I wrap my legs around his hips to keep from falling—which has the delightful side effect of rubbing the shaft of his cock right against my bare pussy. I whimper at the sensation while Egorr hastily carries me down the hall and, managing to hold me up with just one hand, he uses the other to push his door open.

Inside his dark bedroom, Egorr drops me onto a soft bed. Then he flicks on the light and before I know it, he's crouched over me, his huge body dwarfing mine. I don't even get a chance to look around the room first.

Egorr tucks some hair behind my ear before trailing his fingers down the valley between my breasts to the soft swell of my stomach. Finally, he reaches the place where my thighs meet, and his hand nudges between them.

Without needing to be told, I part my legs. Those thick fingers of his swoop lower, and he drags one over my outer lips. I fall back down to the bed at just this small touch. It feels electric. He dips deeper, finding my heat underneath, and groans.

"You're so wet," Egorr says with genuine surprise.

I grin mischievously. "Like I said, you turn me on."

He sweeps my moisture upward, using it to ease his way toward my clit. There, he pauses, and gently brushes over it.

My whole body convulses. He does it again, gentle while applying just enough pressure, and again I respond. Nobody's hand has ever felt so good on me.

After teasing my clit just a little more, he returns lower, where he tests me out with his finger. I'm shocked at how that finger refuses to fit. Egorr exhales sharply.

"Damn," he says, circling my slit, pressing in, then circling again. "You're so small."

"Sorry," I say reflexively. Egorr shakes his head and leans down to kiss me.

"You're human. I think it's expected."

Finally, his finger slips in, and my head falls back onto the bed. Once it's inside me, it's like he's on a waterslide. My hips snap up, drawing it in deeper, and Egorr falls onto his elbow with a heady grunt.

If just his finger is this good inside me, I can't imagine how his cock will feel.

It's not long of him pumping his hand before I get impatient. I want him to fuck me. But Egorr must see the look in my eyes because a grin tilts up his mouth. With his finger still buried in me up to the knuckle, he crawls down the bed and drops his head between my legs.

"Mmm," Egorr hums. "You're so cute down here."

"Cute?"

While he continues sliding his hand in and out, he uses the other to spread my lower lips.

"Cute. All pink and swollen up for me." He licks his lips. "I can't wait to eat you."

When he wedges his face between my legs, his tusks push my thighs apart, cool against my hot skin. His tongue darts out and touches me, and I almost fall back against the bed, but I want to watch him, so I prop myself up on my elbows as Egorr's mouth starts its work on me.

I can't help an undignified moan when he flicks his tongue over my clit. Then again, in the same torturous motion.

"Oh, damn." I'm enthralled by the sight of his big head between my legs, his eyes closed in pleasure. Soon, I'm unable to hold myself up any longer, and I topple back onto the bed as Egorr latches onto that tiny nub and sucks on it. Then he switches back to his tongue, all while he slides that marvelous, thick finger in and out of me.

Already my orgasm is twisting and turning in my hips, winding its way up my spine to my neck. It's chasing me the way Egorr is chasing my clit, circling it with his tongue, pouncing on it and then falling back again to simply tease it. Every time I gasp or moan, he repeats the motion, like he's experimenting to find out what will pleasure me most and then doing it again and again.

Soon I'm writhing on the bed, clenching my thighs together around his head and gripping the blankets as he torments me between the legs.

"Fuck," I moan, the pressure rising higher and higher. Soon I'm going to simply combust. "Egorr! I... I..." I don't know what I want to say, but I can't stop the scrambled thoughts rolling around my brain from coming out of my mouth. I can hear and feel him chuckle against me as he licks harder and pumps his hand faster. "Please, don't stop!"

"I would never," he murmurs.

Then, suddenly, something is widening me—it's a second finger trying to push its way in. As I stretch to accommodate it, my nerve endings are firing on all cylinders. I'm not just moaning anymore but crying out, and then the wave hits me hard.

I scream as my pussy clamps down tight, and still those

fingers are thrusting inside of me while I squeeze and shudder. My back arches as pulse after pulse of pleasure ripples through me.

Eventually Egorr slows his attack, and I wriggle my hips at how overstimulated I am. He releases me, and his fingers make a wet slurping sound as he withdraws them.

I lie there, panting and dumbfounded. I've never experienced an orgasm like that in my entire life.

Egorr sits up and licks his lips. "Wow." He grins with his whole wide mouth. "You make such wonderful sounds."

I have to laugh. "I sounded like a strangled cat."

He falls down to the bed next to me, resting one hand on my belly. When I glance down, I find his huge green cock is even harder than before, and the barely exposed head shines with wetness. Suddenly my hunger for it is a roaring monster. I want that thing inside me, *now*.

Trailing my hands over his big belly, down to his hips, I smooth one over his groin, and Egorr tenses as I reach the thick thatch of black hair there. Interesting that he has no hair on his head, but plenty down here. His cock is reaching out directly toward me, like it wants me just as much. I gently run one hand over it, and Egorr lets out a sharp breath as I slip down and explore further.

Holy shit. He has huge balls, that's for sure. I've never found balls very hot before, but I can barely fit them in my palm, and that cranks up my dial.

Now there's a droplet of white sliding down the underside of his cock, so I snatch it up with the tip of my finger and bring it to my lips. Egorr stares, wide-eyed, as I taste it.

"I want to go down on you, too," I say, relishing the salty, musky flavor of him. Wow. Nobody told me ogre cum tasted *good*. Or maybe that's just Egorr.

He hesitates. "I might go off too soon, and I'd much rather, uh..."

Oh, I see. I grin mischievously.

"Do it inside me?" I ask brightly.

His green cheeks turn an even darker shade of green, and he scratches his big, bald head. Even his pointed ears twitch.

"Well, if you don't want me to suck you like a lollipop, then..."

"I do," Egorr interrupts, his gaze suddenly turning intense. "I do, Maddie. But you tasted so good that now all my cock wants is to fuck you."

I'm probably smiling from ear to ear. Egorr might be a sweet giant on the outside, but he's filthy on the inside, and my affection for him swells even bigger.

"Good," I say, rolling over so I'm facing him. I hook one leg over his hip, so now that enormous thing between his legs is pressing against my pelvis. He's so much bigger than I am that I have to tilt my head up to look at him. "Then do it."

All that sweetness fades from Egorr's face, replaced by determination. He rubs himself harder against me, then reaches down to shove that amazing cock between my legs, the head poking up between my thighs. Holy shit. Just the sensation of that hard, hot object against me instantly sets my skin ablaze. I drag myself over it, sliding along on how slick he's made me, and Egorr groans. His expression is serious and concentrated as he pushes me down to the bed so I'm on my back, then pulls my thighs apart, gripping his cock tight in one huge hand.

"Put it inside me," I say, lifting my hips toward his. "Please."

His lip pulls up on one side. "If she asks so nicely..."

Egorr drags the head through my folds, back and forth over my clit, swirling his pre-cum all around until I'm whining. My pussy tightens around nothing. Egorr stares intently at the space between us as he navigates downward, and I moan, just anticipating how good he'll feel.

Then he presses inside.

I gasp with shock as that huge cock tries to fit into me—and my pussy only allows the tip to squeeze through, halting his progress. Egorr furrows his brow, equally as surprised by my body's resistance.

"You're so tiny," he says, uncertain. "I don't know if it will fit, Maddie."

"It will fit." I gasp and wriggle, trying to bring him back in. I need him. Surely we'll fit together—we're meant to fit together. "Just try again."

Egorr's brow furrows. "If you're sure."

He withdraws and then attempts once more, pushing harder this time. Still, he's too big, and the skin around my entrance can't stretch anymore. I've never taken something this size, even when I played with my toys back at New Eden.

"Egorr," I moan, willing myself to open up for him. "Try again, please."

"I don't know if—"

Suddenly, a fierce bolt of pain tears through me.

"Fuck!" I cry out as that massive, thick cock finally slides through. Egorr freezes, and his face melts in concern.

"Are you okay?" he asks, still only a few centimeters deep. Just his breathing moves his cock inside me, making me whimper in pain.

Oh, fuck, does that hurt. I clench my eyes shut and every muscle in me tenses.

Quickly Egorr pulls out, and I can't stop the tears that rush from my eyes at the searing pain radiating out from between my thighs.

"Shit, shit, shit." I reach down and cover myself with one hand, as if that will help numb the discomfort.

Egorr looks down between my legs, and horror dawns on his face.

"What is it?" I ask, wincing.

"You're bleeding!" Quickly, he gets up from the bed and rushes to the bathroom, and I hear the water running as I try to wipe away my tears. Egorr returns with a wet cloth, his expression filled with worry and regret, and he gently presses it against my torn flesh—which only makes me whimper again.

"I'm so sorry," Egorr says, breathing hard. "I don't know what happened, I—"

But I know what happened. He's way too huge for my much smaller body, and we shouldn't have forced it. *I* shouldn't have forced it.

This is my fault.

I take gasping breaths, trying to stop my crying because I know it won't help right now.

"It's fine," I manage. I pat Egorr's arm, but clench my eyes shut as this small movement makes that aching place between my legs burn brighter. Egorr lies down next to me, his hands poised as if he wants to touch me but he doesn't want to make it worse.

"You're just... you're just big," I say between clenched teeth. "That's all."

"'That's all'?" Egorr's horrified. "I split you, Maddie!" He drags a hand down his face and shakes his head. "This is terrible. I can't believe I did that to you."

"Egorr." I rub his big chest, then lean my head against it. "You didn't know. I didn't know."

I take a few deep, calming breaths. The pain will fade eventually, and my skin will knit itself back together. I finally turn on the bed toward him, squinting.

Egorr wants to say more, apologize more, but I stop him with a finger on his lips.

"Shh." I nuzzle up to him, and he tentatively curls one arm around me. "We just went into it too fast. Which is my fault." I chuckle, and the movement makes me gasp. "I really wanted you inside me."

"Me, too." He sighs heavily. "I'm so sorry."

I reach up to stroke his tusk. "It'll heal. We just might have to, um, wait a while before we can try again."

Egorr nods. "I'll wait as long as I have to."

I lean into his chest. "Good." Then a lovely thought occurs to me. "This means I can suck you off, right?"

Egorr's booming laugh brings a smile to my face.

"I can't believe you're still thinking about me." He pushes some hair away from my eyes. "You don't have to do that, Maddie. You're hurt."

"But I want to."

Moving still makes my torn skin throb like a bitch, but I power through it as I slink down the length of Egorr's body to where his cock now lies rather limp between his legs. I'm sure watching a girl cry is a significant turnoff.

Egorr turns over onto his back uneasily, and I slide my elastic tie off my wrist to pull my hair out of the way. Then I wrap my hands around the rather significant girth of him and gently stroke. Under my palms, Egorr hardens right up again.

Perfect. It's a tight fit, but I do manage to get his huge cock between my lips, and I love the deep groan I earn as I bring as much as I can into my mouth. I circle the head with my tongue, experimenting to see what he likes while I keep one hand rooted to the base of his cock, which is rapidly hardening in my hands.

Damn. It's too bad this thing couldn't fit inside me, because it's wonderful. He's soft and rigid in all the right ways, and feels so smooth under my fingers. He tastes like heaven. I apply suction as I slide him in deep again, and Egorr's hips jerk up into my mouth. His gasps and moans are all the reward I need as I take him as far in as I can.

It only takes a few strong sucks before he tenses up all over, and his huge cock swells in my palms. He mutters, "Maddie!" just before he unleashes inside my mouth, filling it completely. I can't even swallow his cum as fast as he's giving it to me, and it spills down my lips.

When I'm finished and my mouth is coated in his rather plentiful spend, Egorr stares down at me.

"Damn," he whispers, eyes wide. "That was amazing."

"Buckle up," I say, wincing a little when I move to cuddle up beside him. "You're gonna be getting these for a while, and I'll only get better at it."

Instead of snuggling, though, Egorr gestures for me to lie back.

"We need to treat that," he says, eyes downcast. "And we should probably take you to a doctor tomorrow, in case you need stitches."

I clench reflexively at the idea of someone stitching me down *there*.

"We don't need to do all that." I screw up my lips. "It will heal on its own."

Egorr doesn't answer as he heads to the bathroom, then returns with a tube of antibacterial salve. He *tsks* as he applies it, and while I wince at the pain, I can see him berating himself silently. When he at last returns to snuggling me, he's tense all over.

"Egorr." I stroke his bare head. "Are you all right?"

"You're asking *me*?" He sighs and rests his cheek between my bare breasts. "I'm worried. What if I did permanent damage?"

"You didn't. I'm sure of it." I hug him tighter against me. "It will be all right."

But lying next to him tonight certainly isn't going to help me keep my hands off him.

"I'm going to go to bed, okay?"

Egorr raises his head. "All right. Thank you for..." He gestures down at his cock.

"Don't thank me." I kiss him square on the lips, holding on to one of his tusks. "I loved it."

I climb off the bed, each movement of my thighs making the wound flare with pain.

"Maddie?" Egorr asks, sitting up. He looks sadder than I wanted to leave him.

"Yes?"

"Sleep well."

I almost don't want to go with how sweet and soft he looks, naked on his bed, but I know that it's good for us to have our own spaces while we're getting to know each other.

"You too, Egorr." I bounce back one more time to drop a kiss on his lips, and he smiles as I head out the door.

Chapter Eight

The next day, the moment I get out of bed, I'm hurting again.

This sucks. I wish I hadn't been so overeager last night. I hurried us, and now the mistake rests on me. I should have known he'd be too big—I'm human and he's an ogre. Of course we aren't made to fit together.

That troubling thought follows me as I hobble out into the living room to find Egorr making breakfast. I thought he would be gone at the office today, so I'm pleased to see him.

He turns around when I appear and a big smile takes over his face.

"Maddie!" He's about to throw his arms around me, but pauses before touching me. "How are you feeling?"

"I'm okay." I don't want to worry him even more, so I put on a happy face. "It hurts a little, but I'm okay."

When I lean into his chest, Egorr hugs me tight. He feels so good and warm that I don't want to let him go.

"Weren't you supposed to go into the office today?" I ask, still buried in him.

"I took the morning off and made a call. Doctor's appointment is at eleven. They were able to squeeze us in."

I shudder. I don't want to visit a doctor about this—it's humiliating.

"Do we have to?" I whine, finally pulling away.

But Egorr's voice is surprisingly firm. "Yes. We need to know if it's serious, and how we can help you heal better." Then his hand trails down and squeezes my butt. "The faster you heal, the sooner we can try again. Right?"

I sigh, which blows a lock of hair away from my face. "Fine. I'll go." He already knows exactly which of my buttons to push to get what he wants. Of course I want to try again. I want to show him that we *can* fit, if we just work at it.

Egorr leans down to kiss my forehead, then realizes the bacon is burning and quickly hurries back to the stovetop to take it off. I sit at the small chair Egorr got for me, and he brings breakfast to the table.

Mornings here are the best.

"Sorry you're missing work today," I say, reaching across the table to rub the top of his big hand. He flips it over so he can twine our fingers together.

"It's no problem. Really."

Once we've eaten, we snuggle on the couch until it's time to head to the doctor's. I'm nervous as we get into the car, and I don't look forward to explaining exactly how we ended up here.

Egorr glances at me as we drive. "I'll be with you the whole time," he says as we pull up to a red light, and he rubs my knee. "If you want that."

I grip his hand. "Yes! Please don't leave me."

He chuckles and puts on the gas as the light turns green. "Don't worry. I'll never leave you."

I don't know if it's what he intends, but I can almost hear

forever behind his words, and it gives me more confidence for what lies ahead.

Finally, we're in the doctor's office. Egorr checks us in at the front desk, and then we sit down to wait.

The room is full of other monsters—a pregnant gargoyle, a swamp monster with a slimy swamp child, and on the far end, a large dragon who seems to have a cold. Every single one of them stares at us when Egorr wraps an arm around me, as if a mythical creature has stepped into their midst. I shrink back against his side, not used to all those eyes on me.

"It's all right," Egorr murmurs into my ear as he leans my head against his big chest.

I don't think anyone is going to hurt me, but I like hiding in his side anyway so I can avoid their curious looks. Right now, I feel too vulnerable. Too *human*.

Finally, the nurse comes out and calls my name. She doesn't hide her surprised expression as Egorr takes my hand and leads me through the door.

We're deposited in one of the clinician rooms, and the nurse asks me to take off my pants and put on a hospital gown. Once I'm appropriately dressed, I lie down on the padded table. I already know this is going to be painfully awkward.

"Don't worry." Egorr rubs my hand where he sits beside the table. "I'm here."

Eventually, the doctor joins us. She's almost human-sized, but much taller thanks to her furry faun legs and black hooves. She has two small horns poking out of her hair, and a little tail flicks behind her as she introduces herself to us, shaking my hand and then Egorr's.

"So tell me what happened," she says, sitting down on a stool at the foot of the bed.

I swallow hard. "Well, I was a little too excited..."

"This is my fault," Egorr interrupts. "I should have gone slower."

I shoot him a chastising look, but he just shakes his head. I don't want him to take this on himself, but I guess I can't stop him now.

The faun doctor waves a hand at both of us. "It's no one's fault. These things happen." She smiles at me. "Are you doing a trial marriage, then?"

I'm surprised by the personal question. "Yeah. I just moved in a few days ago."

"Well, see? You couldn't have known. This is all new to you." She gently taps my knee. "Can you open your legs for me, Maddie? So I can take a look?"

I blush madly as I part my knees and let her peer under the hospital gown. She brings out a light and examines between my thighs, making a little *hmm* sound.

"A perineal tear," she pronounces, sliding her stool back. She taps my knee once more. "You can close up."

I press my legs back together with relief.

"What's a perineal tear?" I ask. "What do we do about it?"

"It's not major. No stitches required, if that's what you were worried about."

Oh, thank goodness. I don't think I could manage through that.

The doctor takes off her gloves. "But it will take a little time to heal, probably four to six weeks."

"*Weeks?*" I gape at her. "Really? But that's such a long time!" I give Egorr a helpless look. I can't wait a month or more, not with how painfully, wonderfully horny he makes me.

"You need to be fully healed before you try again. And... there are some things you can do to help it along."

The doctor proceeds to outline the care instructions for us. "If it hurts, use an ice pack." She types on her computer while she talks. "Sit in warm water three times a day, and use baby wipes when you go to the restroom. Walking and moderate exercise are fine, but avoid anything too strenuous, and don't lift any heavy objects."

"I can handle the lifting," Egorr says with a wink.

"But really?" I ask, the pitch of my voice rising. "A whole month?"

The faun nods, her expression serious. "Otherwise you could reopen the wound. Let it rest." She glances between us. "You'll have to get creative in the meantime."

I blush furiously at this suggestion, but Egorr just chuckles.

"I think we can do that," he murmurs to me, and a sharp tingle races down my spine.

"But next time..." The doctor gives each of us a stern look. "Go slower. You may even consider a dilator so this doesn't happen again in the future."

I blink. "A dilator?"

"It's a device that you can use daily to stretch your vagina."

I cringe at the word. "Oh."

I suppose that will help us be more prepared next time— but I'm disappointed that we'll have to wait even longer. I wish I weren't so small. Egorr probably didn't have this problem with the bigfoot he dated before me.

"We'll get one right away," Egorr says, and when he smiles down at me, I just want to kiss his big lips. And then do even filthier things to him.

This is going to be a very long, very rough month.

Egorr drops me off at home, and I lean through the car window to kiss him hard before he pulls away to head to work for the afternoon.

As instructed, I fill the bathtub with warm water, then sit in it for a good twenty minutes. It hurts like a bitch at first, but eventually the water becomes soothing rather than irritating. Then I read a book for the rest of the day, already making a mental list of things Egorr and I can do outside of vaginal pene-tration to stave off my irrepressible needs.

I guess if this had to happen with anyone, I'm glad it happened with someone as kind and relaxed as Egorr. He wasn't perturbed in the least by our appointment, and it brings me immense relief. This could have been monumentally awkward with anyone else.

But that doesn't wipe away the disappointment—nor how inadequate I feel.

Finally, the door opens, and Egorr steps into the house. I'm so relieved to see him that I hop off the couch and throw myself at him, arms wide, even though it makes everything hurt. He chuckles as he brings me in for a hug, squeezing me against his big body, then leans down to kiss the top of my head.

"I'm happy to see you, too," he says as I tilt my chin up toward him. He gives me a big fat kiss on my lips, which stirs up all that warm lust that's been bubbling inside me since our failed attempt. I sink deeper into him, winding my arms around his neck and standing up on my toes so we can be even closer.

It only takes a few seconds of voraciously kissing for the bulge under his jeans to make itself known. Egorr's hands roam my sides, over my hips, around my back and down to my ass. There he squeezes, and I let out a hum of pleasure into his mouth.

"Maddie," he finally says, breaking away. "Are you hungry?"

The question takes me by surprise. "Well, yes." I trail my hand down his belly to the lump between his thighs, and Egorr's eyes fall closed. "For this."

"But, dinner—"

"Dinner can wait a few minutes, can't it?" I stroke harder, and Egorr's breath hitches. I search for the button on his jeans, and then the zipper before I tug them down. His cock is stretching the fabric of his boxers already, and it's almost too big to be contained by them. I slide a finger under the band and pull those down, too, until that huge, green cock springs out, eagerly growing thicker in front of me.

When I wrap a hand around it, Egorr grunts.

"Maddie, you don't have to do that," he says, though his voice is strained as I steadily stroke him.

"Of course not." I grin. "But I want to, more than anything."

His eyes are wide as he nods. I get down on my knees, and they grow even bigger as I lean forward and bring him into my mouth.

He tastes salty and musky, perfectly male, and I groan with pleasure as I suck him in deeper. Egorr is panting as I slide him out again, my hand moving in tandem with my lips, and then sink him back into my mouth. His whole body jerks as I swallow more, then even more, until the soft head strikes the back of my throat.

His big hand settles around the back of my head. "Maddie," he groans, and it's utterly erotic that he makes that sound for me. "That's incredible."

I giggle against him, which vibrates my mouth around his cock, and Egorr lets out an even more tortured sound. While I'm sucking him like a lollipop, I venture downward with my other hand, exploring the heavy sac hanging beneath. I cup one of his balls in my palm and gently massage it.

Egorr reaches out and grabs the edge of the nearby desk. "Oh, shit, I'm going to—"

That's all it takes to send him over the edge. Warm fluid

coats the inside of my mouth, filling it full before I have to start swallowing.

When I look up at Egorr, he's gaping down at me.

"Wow." He takes my hands to help me up to my feet, then wipes some of his cum away from my chin. "That was incredible."

"Good. You taste amazing, and I love your moans."

His green face turns an even darker, ruddier shade of green. "Oh. I've never... No one's ever said that to me before."

I head to the counter to get a towel to wipe off my face, while Egorr puts his pants back on.

"No, no," I say, flapping a hand. "You're home. Doesn't that mean it's sweatpants time?"

He shakes his head. "You said you hadn't gone out to eat yet, right? So I thought that's what we should do. Have a nice dinner, and then..." He bites his lip. "You know. Talk about what things we might want to do while you're healing."

I brighten immediately. "Do you mean *sex* things?"

I love Egorr's booming laugh. "Yes, like that." He nods to where our jackets are hanging on the wall by the door. "So? What do you think?"

"Going out sounds great." I love how easy that is to say here in the real world. We get to do things like *go out*—whenever we want. "Let me put on something cuter, though? I thought we were going to stay in, so I'm not dressed up."

Egorr grins widely as he makes himself comfortable in a chair. "Can't wait to see it."

Chapter Nine

*O*nce I'm all dolled up, we decide to grab dinner at a pub close by that Egorr claims has "amazing fish and chips." He gifts me with an appreciative grin when I emerge from my bedroom, and he runs his finger through one of the curls I put in my hair.

"You look gorgeous." He kisses me, and then we hop in the car and head out.

The pub is a cute place tucked into the corner of an old building, and it's surprisingly busy. Once we slide into an open booth, each of us orders a beer, and I pick something dark and malty to enjoy with my food.

It's exciting to be out and about somewhere so... animated. The bar is packed full of monsters chatting and laughing—a griffon, a manticore, and what appears to be a giant. There are a handful of pool tables, and nearby, an ogress and a lion man are throwing darts.

It's like something out of a television show, a world that only existed as fiction while I lived on the preserve. Now, I'm coming to find out it's all very real. The world is so much bigger than I thought.

But today I'm painfully aware of one thing: how much smaller and weaker I am. I hadn't been quite so self-conscious before, but after our bedroom misadventure, now I can't help thinking of how much more appropriate any of these other, much larger monsters would be as Egorr's partner.

Some of my enthusiasm about going out fades. Sure, there are lots of fun things we can do without, quote, *vaginal penetration*, but that was a lot of the fun stuff. And now, because of me, it's going to be a whole month at least before we can try again.

After we've placed our orders for food, I notice the ogress playing darts is watching us with a sideways smile on her face.

"Hey," she says, sidling over to our table. She's completely focused on Egorr, as if she's greeting only him. "What's your name?"

I balk. Egorr, too, seems startled at the stranger approaching us.

"Egorr," he answers automatically.

She extends her hand to shake, and after a moment's hesitation, he takes it. Where Egorr's big hand dwarfs mine, theirs are about evenly matched.

"Do you want to play darts with us?" the ogress asks. "My friend is beating me handily, and I want to show him ogres aren't all slouches."

I suppose that's why she's here talking to Egorr in the first place. He did say there aren't many ogres in the world, so this must be a pretty uncommon circumstance.

Egorr glances over at me, then back up at the ogress.

"I'm not very good at darts, either," he says amiably. "Well, I haven't really tried."

"Come on, just give it a go." She winks. "You might be a pro and you don't even know it yet."

I'm silently asking Egorr to turn her down. We're here to hang out together and eat dinner, not to play darts with strangers. I can tell, though, that he's undecided.

"All right," Egorr says eventually, standing up. My heart sinks. "But my girlfriend wants to play, too, right? Maddie?"

I swallow down how annoyed I feel, because I want to be a good, fun girlfriend, not a stick in the mud.

"Sure."

Maybe it won't be so bad, and I'm just being territorial. We could even make some friends, as I don't get the sense Egorr has many of those.

The ogress gives me a flat smile. "We can all play," she agrees. Then she offers Egorr a handful of darts, held together with a rubber band, and nods to the dartboard. "Let's show this lion what ogres are made of, huh?"

Egorr gets up and I follow to join them in front of the dartboards. As a side thought, the ogress hands me a bundle of darts, too, and her eyes glaze over me like I'm not even there.

I thought monsters out in the world would be scary—not rude. But I have to remember Egorr doesn't see his own kind much, and this could be good for him.

The lion man crosses his arms and leans against the wall while Egorr lines up with the dartboard, aiming his first dart. He throws it, and it bounces right off the board.

The ogress chuckles. "You have to put a little more force behind it," she says. She steps up next to throw, and her dart hits near the outside of the dartboard.

The lion man tallies her score on a chalkboard, and then it's my turn. While I aim my dart, I hear the ogress talking to Egorr.

"So, what do you do for work?"

"Oh, uh, I'm a computer guy."

"What sort of computer guy?"

Egorr's about to answer when I throw the dart, and I put

my entire arm behind it. Just this movement makes the ache between my legs burn, but I'm not going to let that stop me. To my surprise, my dart lodges itself in the dartboard on the skinny ring closest to the bullseye, on the red wedge marked with a "20."

The lion man lets out a whistle. "Wow. Sixty points on her first throw!" He gives me a nod of approval. "Not bad."

The ogress is still too busy talking to Egorr to notice my high score. I prickle all over at how close she's standing to him as they chit chat. But they probably have a lot in common, that's all. More than Egorr and I do.

I grab my beer and take a big gulp, hoping the alcohol will calm me down, because heat is spreading rapidly across my body. I'm embarrassed and irritated at the same time.

"My turn," the lion man announces, though I'm the only one paying attention to him. When he throws, he hits in the wedge marked with a "6."

"Damn." With a shake of his head, he adds our scores to the chalkboard.

The ogress is next, and she, too, doesn't hit the board.

She giggles. "Gosh, I'm really bad at this," she says to Egorr. "You have to reclaim my honor."

Egorr gives a noncommittal chuckle, and picks up his next dart. "I will try to restore the reputation of ogres."

I wish Egorr would talk to *me* instead. We were supposed to be here as a couple, to spend time together, but now some stranger has all his attention.

The lion man rolls his eyes as Egorr takes up position and throws again. This time, it lands, though only in the wedge marked "2."

"Good try," the ogress says, smacking Egorr playfully on the arm. That heat is spreading into my face, and now my vague frustration is morphing into anger. She's clearly flirting with him, and he hasn't done anything to stop her.

I don't even know if he's noticed—and if he has, he doesn't seem to mind.

Thankfully, that's when our food arrives. I surrender the rest of the game so I can go back to our table and eat, and hopefully return to having our nice dinner out.

"Aww," the ogress says to Egorr when he turns around to join me. "You're not going to give up yet, are you?"

He glances between me and her, and I stare into my food, my heart beating faster. Surely he's going to choose me and give up this silly game.

I should say something. I should ask him to sit and eat with me. But I want *him* to choose that, to decide he'd prefer to spend his time with me. I shouldn't have to make him.

"It'll only take a few more minutes," the ogress presses. "The game's almost done."

I stare at my food, too shaky to even pick up my fork. When I remain silent, Egorr sighs.

"All right, we'll just finish out the game."

I want to scream into my fish and chips as they return to the game and the ogress takes her turn. This time she hits close to the bullseye, and Egorr congratulates her.

While he steps up to take his next throw, the lion man sits down across from me.

"It's too bad you gave up," he says. "You had a killer score going."

My shoulders curl forward. "Yeah. Whatever." I couldn't care less about my score. All I can see is red as Egorr hurls his next dart, and the ogress crows.

"Good throw!" she says, slapping him on the back.

I want to crawl into a hole and die. He still hasn't told her off, and now I'm starting to wonder if maybe he likes her back.

Maybe he hasn't said anything because he really doesn't mind the attention of another ogre.

The lion man extends a big paw across the table toward me. "I'm Astor, by the way."

Not wanting to be rude—and feeling a little uncertain now that Egorr's left me completely in the hands of another monster —I reluctantly take it and shake. Astor holds on to my hand for much too long, so quickly I withdraw mine.

"I don't see many humans out here in the world." Astor cocks his head. "And I've definitely never met one in person."

"Yeah," I say noncommittally. "We're doing a trial marriage."

His eyebrows rise up into his big, fluffy mane. "Oh, really?" Then he frowns at Egorr and the ogress, who are now chatting as they add up their scores. My skin feels like a raging inferno, and every one of my muscles has gone tense. "Doesn't look like he's married to you from where I'm sitting."

There's a pitying look on the lion man's face as he picks up a few of Egorr's fries and eats them.

"Maybe after he sends you back to the preserve, you should do a trial marriage with me instead?" Astor asks with a grin. "I certainly wouldn't be off flirting with someone else when I had a sweet little human waiting for me."

After he sends me back? Egorr and the ogress are still locked in conversation, and tears sting my eyes.

It all makes sense. If he'd tried to have sex with someone like her instead, this wouldn't have happened. Egorr would never have torn someone his own size. Maybe he was kind to me at the doctor's office, but what if I'm really not suited to him? What if we can *never* have sex, and then he does take me back to New Eden?

That's the last straw. I refuse to be returned again. If Egorr is going to send me back, I want it to be on *my* terms, not his.

I get up and stalk over to Egorr. He turns to me, smiling, but it quickly fades when he sees my murderous expression.

"You," I say, glaring at the ogress. "I don't know what you think you're doing, but it's fucking rude." Her mouth falls open in surprise as I turn my gaze on Egorr. "And you? I thought..." The tears are coming now, and I can't stop them. "I thought we had something. I really did."

"What?" His eyes are wide. "Maddie? What do you mean?"

My temper flares even bigger. Is he really that clueless? Despite what he said when we first met, I think he's attracted to this ogress and doesn't even realize it.

I don't care if I'm not supposed to be alone. I can't stand looking at Egorr's face a moment longer, and my temper has unfurled into something big and terrible. The last thing I want is to say something even worse than I already have, so I spin around and stomp out of the pub.

"Maddie!"

Tears rushing down my cheeks, the door falls closed behind me with a *slam!*

Out in the sunshine, I jog down the street, wanting to get as far away as possible from that scene. I have no idea where I'm going, but I want to be anywhere else.

"Maddie!" I hear Egorr call after me. I speed up, running around a right corner, where I keep going, too full of rage and hurt to stop. "Maddie, wait!"

I turn my head to see him chasing after me. But while I'm looking away, I collide with something rather hard.

Stone hard.

Wincing with pain, I glance up, only to find myself standing hip-level with a huge, towering rock giant. It stares down at me.

"A human?" A smile spreads across its face. "Wow. I

haven't seen a human in a long time." It reaches down, and even as I try to back away, its arms are much too long for me to escape. It seizes me around the middle and lifts me up into the air.

I scream. The rock giant smiles wider.

"So small," it says, bringing me close to its face to study me. "How cute."

I'm going to die. This is how I die. Eaten by a rock giant because I was stupid and ran off on my own.

"Hey!" It's Egorr below me, shouting angrily. "Put her down!"

The giant tilts its head. Egorr looks ready to throw himself into the huge creature's leg like a linebacker.

"What?" my captor says with an annoyed grunt. "Is this yours?"

I want him to say *yes*. *Yes, she's mine.*

Instead Egorr says, "You're going to hurt her. Let her go." He readies his fists, and even though he's big, I'm not sure how well he would fare against a twelve-foot monster made of solid stone.

"Jeez," the rock giant says, lowering me to the ground again. "Sorry."

With a huff, it drops me onto the sidewalk. Then it strides on past us, grumbling as it goes by.

I sit there on the cement on my ass, tears of anger and fear rushing down my cheeks. Egorr kneels beside me, his expression panicked.

"Are you okay?" he asks, putting a hand on my shoulder. I shove him away, and he looks even more surprised.

"Leave me alone!" I crawl back to my feet and dust off my knees, trying to pretend I'm not terrified out of my skin. I might have almost just died.

"What happened?" Egorr asks, keeping his distance this time, but his expression is worried. "Why did you run?"

I round on him, all my fear turning into frustration.

"Because you don't want me!" I feverishly wipe my face with my arm as more tears drip down my cheeks. "We're all wrong for each other!"

"What?" His mouth falls open. "What do you mean?"

"I want to go home. Take me back to New Eden. Right now."

The surprise on his face fades into devastation.

"Oh." Egorr fumbles like he's trying to find words. "If that's really what you want..." He clenches one hand into a fist and stares down at the ground.

"It is."

It's not. I wanted him to choose me. I wanted to be right for him, but this is just Shisek all over again. I should go back to the preserve now, before Egorr realizes what a mistake he made taking me home with him.

This time, I want to be the one who says how it ends.

With a slow nod, Egorr turns around and starts walking back to the pub. I follow behind him, trying to stifle my angry tears. He opens the car door for me and I slide in, then grab the handle and slam it closed. Still silent, Egorr goes inside to pay our tab, and while he's gone, I yank out my phone to call the resident director. I'm going to tell her I'm on my way back, that things haven't worked out.

But before I can hit "dial," the driver's side door opens again and Egorr gets in. He doesn't start the car, though. He just sits there, looking out the windshield, his lower lip trembling.

"What happened in there?" he asks, keeping his eyes fixed on the road, blinking rapidly. "What did I do?"

"It's a matter of what you *didn't* do!" I can't believe he

doesn't see it. "You just let that ogre lady fawn all over you. You could have told her off, you could have sat down with me and eaten dinner together, but *no*. You had to finish the stupid game. You had to keep talking to her when I was right there waiting for you!"

I'm panting by the time I'm finished, so full of hurt and anger and rejection that I'm shaking. Egorr turns to me, and it's as if some great realization has dawned on him.

"I'm sorry," he says. His eyes are red. "I'm so sorry, Maddie. You're right. I should have said 'no.' I don't know what's wrong with me."

"It's fine," I grind out. "I understand. We're not a good fit."

In more ways than one.

"I..." Egorr suddenly hits the steering wheel with his fists. "I have to take you back if you say that's what you want. Those are the rules." I realize now, from the cracking in his voice, that he's crying, too. "But I would hate doing it. I want to go home with you. Back to *our* home. I want to..." He sniffles, interrupting himself. "There are so many more things I wanted to do with you."

Something about seeing this giant ogre cry makes me break inside. My anger morphs into sadness and regret.

"Why?" I ask, sniffling. "Why did you let her flirt with you like that? Why didn't you stand up for me?"

"I don't know. I didn't want to be rude to another ogre. I... I didn't realize I was hurting you." Egorr reaches out like he wants to touch me but stops himself. "I'm sorry. I should have put spending time with you first."

"Yeah." I cross my arms over my chest. "You should have."

"Please don't go back to New Eden." This time, Egorr does take my hand in his, and I let him because as upset as I am, I still crave his touch. "Give me another shot, Maddie. I promise I won't mess it up again."

I see how his cheeks are still wet with tears and sigh. He really is clueless. Not malicious, just clueless, and too nice for his own good.

And maybe that's one of the things I like about him.

"Okay," I say eventually, rubbing my eyes, which are now dry and sandy from crying. "Let's go back to your house."

With a relieved nod, Egorr puts the car in drive.

Chapter Ten

*W*hen we arrive back at the cute little door in the hillside, neither of us speaks. Egorr opens it for me, and though the fire has died inside, it's still lovely and warm. I just need to be alone for a while to sort through what happened, so I head to my room and shut myself in.

I think about calling Celeste for some comfort, but I don't want to have to tell her all the sordid details. Maybe I did over-react, and I don't want her to judge me. Besides, Egorr apologized. That's good enough, right?

I lie back on the bed, trying to sort through the conflicting feelings roiling inside me. My wounds from Shisek are still too fresh not to take it personally. I can't bear the idea of being rejected again. I need to feel like I'm enough.

When I finally walk into the living room, Egorr's in the kitchen. I smell something absolutely lovely.

"What's that?" I ask, and he spins around, surprised by the sound of my voice. He smiles bigger than I've ever seen him smile, like he can't believe I'm still here.

"Chicken parmesan," he says, stirring something in a pan.

"And homemade marinara to go on top." He quickly opens a bottle of wine, then pulls down two glasses and fills them. "I know it's late, but we didn't eat dinner, so..."

Oh, wow. He's really pulling out all the stops. I take an uneasy seat on one of the stools at the island, and Egorr slides the glass in front of me.

"Maddie..." he begins.

I hold up a hand. "I want to forget it ever happened."

He furrows his brow, then shakes his head. "No. We need to talk about it."

Egorr walks around the island and sits down at the stool next to me.

"I want you," he says, with a surprising sternness. "I want you more than anything. More than anyone else. And I'll do whatever it takes for you to believe that."

Ugh, I'm not going to cry again today.

"I think it'll just take time," I say quietly, swishing my wine glass to hide my unsteady hand. "I..." I swallow hard. I need to tell him why it hurt me so much. Why what happened tonight hit me in the place where I'm most tender.

"What is it?" Egorr asks, his expression open and ready to listen.

"You know I was sent back." I try to still the rapid beating of my heart as I expose my weakness to him. Egorr just nods, waiting for what I have to say next. "I wasn't enough for him. I wasn't the right fit. He... he wanted something else, someone more like him."

Someone who didn't need furniture, for starters. Probably someone who wasn't as needy as I am.

"I like you, Egorr," I say with a sniffle. "And I want to be enough. But today made me feel like I wasn't. Like maybe you need someone else, after... you know." I rub my face with one hand, and my voice drops quieter. "When we didn't fit."

Egorr's brows rise, and I think he finally understands. Shaking his head, he rests his hand over mine.

"I'm so sorry I made you feel that way," he says in a tender voice, his eyes so full of emotion it makes me feel like crying again. "You are enough, Maddie. You're the one I need more than anything, the one I want to share my home with me. You're so wonderful that I feel like I don't deserve you."

"What?" I'm affronted. "Why would you think that?"

"Because you're fun. And outgoing. And really, really beautiful." He lets out a self-deprecating laugh. "What beautiful human wants an ogre? An ogre who lives alone and is, apparently, utterly clueless?"

I gape at him. "But I do want you." I turn my hand over and wrap my fingers around his. "Truly, I do."

"Even though I hurt you?" he asks, voice turning sad. "In more ways than one."

"I think we were both a little clueless in the bedroom. You're, um... very well-endowed." I blush as I say it.

He blinks, then smiles.

"I think I'm normal for an ogre. But once you're healed, we'll be more careful." He leans down to kiss my forehead. "And that doesn't mean anything about how suited we are for each other. It will just take time."

The oven beeps, and Egorr gets up and grabs an oven mitt to take the chicken out. It smells incredible. After he serves up the chicken parmesan, I get completely engrossed in my food.

"This is fucking amazing," I say, shoving another forkful into my mouth. "Do you cook like this all the time?"

Egorr shrugs. "I try. Though there's not a lot of reason to cook anything fancy when I live alone."

I wipe my lips with a napkin. "Well, I guess now that you're not living alone, you can cook fancy all the time."

He laughs, and it's a booming, lovely laugh, that feels like maybe we've gotten through the worst of it.

"I'd like that."

After we've cleaned up dinner, we settle down on the couch in front of the fire. Egorr spreads his legs and offers me a seat between them, and I grab my book before settling in. I lean back against his big chest, and he pulls down a blanket to cover both of us.

We spend the rest of the evening curled up together, Egorr's big breaths calming my unsteady heart. He pauses his reading from time to time to smooth a hand down my hair and leave a kiss on the crown of my head. Before I know it, I'm asleep in his arms, my book forgotten on the floor.

I barely register when Egorr picks me up and carries me back to my room. He pulls aside the blankets and sets me gently on the bed, and I mumble a little at the loss of his warmth when he brings the sheets up to my chin.

"Good night," he murmurs, pecking my cheek. "I'll see you in the morning. And then we'll do so many fun things together."

I fall asleep imagining what those things might be.

The next day, Egorr has to go back into the office, but I wake up early to him kissing me on the forehead.

"Little Maddie," he hums, pushing some hair back from my face. "I'll see you tonight, all right? And this time we'll go somewhere nice."

"Mmm," I manage to say back, and he chuckles. Then, with one more kiss to my lips, Egorr gets up and leaves the room, and I quickly fall back asleep.

Later, when I'm finally awake enough to get out of bed, I

follow the routine of getting in the warm water and waiting impatiently, just like the doctor ordered. I have a video chat with Celeste that afternoon, and we talk all about her latest applications, and what life with Egorr's been like. Then I broach the subject of what happened at the pub.

Celeste frowns when I tell her the whole story.

"You ran off on your own? Something a lot worse could have happened to you, Maddie!"

"That's what you're focusing on?" I pout.

"It sounds like Egorr struggles with social situations." Celeste gives me a pitying look. "You were right to be upset, but he apologized and promised to do better, right?"

"Yeah, he did." I hunch forward. "We talked it out, and I do feel better, but..."

Celeste nods like she already understands. "But some trust was lost, wasn't it?"

I nod, transparent as a window, as always.

She sighs. "I'm sorry. I understand."

"But it's okay." I hastily wave my hands. "We're going out to dinner tonight somewhere upscale. Then Egorr promised me 'fun things' at home."

My best friend grins. "I'm glad you found someone as horny as you are."

I snort.

When four o'clock rolls around, I start dressing up for tonight. I wonder where Egorr's going to take me this time. It better not be a pub.

The door finally opens around five, and when Egorr steps inside and sees me, a big smile lights up his face. I throw myself at him, not realizing how much I missed him in the hours he was gone. Ever since I saw him cry yesterday, all I want is to make him smile again.

He hugs me back, completely wrapping me up in his thick arms.

"It's good to see you, too," Egorr says before releasing me. His eyes travel from my face down to my toes, then back up again, and he seems immensely pleased. "You look wonderful. I'm going to clean up and then we can go. I got reservations for six."

I rock forward on my heels in excitement. "Reservations? Must be a nice restaurant."

He shrugs, but a grin pulls at his cheek as he heads to his bedroom to change. When he emerges again, he's in a sexy polo shirt and a pair of slacks that look wonderful on him—though I think I like Egorr in just about any state of dress.

At the front door, he takes my hand. "Ready?"

I squeeze his fingers tight. "Ready."

Egorr drives us into the city, and parks along Central Avenue in the downtown district. When we get out of the car, I'm shocked to find just how many monsters are walking up and down the street. I've never been anywhere so crowded.

I wrap my hand around Egorr's arm, staying close to his side as we navigate onto the sidewalk, toward the restaurant. We step in behind a minotaur couple and wait until it's our turn with the host. Then we're led to our table—a cute little two-seater with a candle sitting in the middle.

"Get whatever you want," Egorr says with a wink. "The plates are small, so we should over-order."

Well, don't mind if I do.

I order pretty much everything on the menu that sounds delicious, and Egorr nods and grins until the fairy waitress starts to look worried.

"Anything else?" she asks as if she doesn't want to know the answer.

Egorr pipes up. "A bottle of wine, please."

Then we hand over our menus. The waitress nods and flits away, half-walking and half-flying. It seems like a perilous thing to do in a restaurant, but she easily dodges a waiter coming the other direction and vanishes into the back room.

We chat companionably about Egorr's day, and I tell him about talking with Celeste. I avoid what happened yesterday, though, because I don't want to ruin the good mood. But I'm still thinking about what she said—how we need to regain trust between us again—and I think this is a good first step.

Then the food arrives, and it's all I can think about. The table is packed full of goodies, from sea scallops in a creamy sauce to bone marrow whipped and served inside the original bone.

"This is incredible," I say, mouth full of food. "It must be costing you a fortune, Egorr."

He shrugs. "I don't spend a lot of money, and I live pretty modestly. I finished paying off my mortgage last year, which is one of the reasons I decided to finally apply for you."

I cock my head. "Oh?"

"It felt like my life was stable enough, and..." He sighs. "I don't think what happened yesterday is the first time I've been oblivious to what my partner needs. I've been alone for a long time, probably for that reason."

I'm surprised that he's broaching the subject, but I continue listening.

"So when I paid off the house and found I was living there all by myself, it was a big moment of realization for me." Egorr looks wistful. "I knew I didn't want to be alone anymore."

"And that's why you applied for me?"

"Yep. So I went to the New Eden website and saw you there, and I guess I just knew."

I lean forward on the table, the delicious food momentarily forgotten. "You knew what?"

"That you were the one for me." He smiles cautiously. "Your little note was so cute and fun and sweet, then I looked at your picture, and it was obvious to me that you were perfect."

I'm swooning so hard I could just fall right out of my chair.

I understand exactly where he's coming from. I understand that deep loneliness, like you're supposed to be at someone's side, but that someone is missing.

Maybe I could be that someone for Egorr, and maybe he could be that someone for me.

"I'm sorry I ran off last night," I say, taking a bite of the whipped bone marrow because I can't keep myself from devouring what's in front of me.

Egorr lets out a heavy breath. "I thought that rock giant was going to squish you. I've never been so scared in my life."

"I thought it was the end for me, too." I slide my hand toward him around the many plates on our table, and Egorr takes it in his much larger palm. "I promise I won't do it again."

"And I promise I won't give you a reason to," he says in return, rubbing my palm with his big thumb.

After dinner, I have to practically waddle back out to the car because of how much I've eaten. Egorr belly laughs as he helps me into the passenger seat, then takes us home back to the hill.

Chapter Eleven

J'm practically falling asleep by the time we pull into the driveway. Egorr suggests that we relax on the couch to digest, and I tumble easily into his lap with a book. But as we read together in front of the fire, his big thighs wrapped around me, there's a growing heat low in my abdomen. I shift a few times to get comfortable, which has the side-effect of rubbing my butt over his crotch.

Soon a rather fat lump is pressing at my ass. There's almost nothing I want more than that cock in my mouth again, aside from that cock being inside me, which isn't an option right now.

"Maddie." Egorr lowers his head so his lips are right by my ear, his tusks getting tangled in my hair. "Do you have any idea how much you turn me on?"

I wiggle a little more against his groin, and he grunts in response.

"I think I have an idea," I hum, relishing the feel of him getting hard for me. "We could do something about it, if you want."

I tilt my head back to look at him, and Egorr's eyes are wide.

"Are you sure?" he asks, a surprising shyness in his voice. "I don't want to push you after... you know."

On the contrary, maybe some intimacy between us would be healing. I want to feel close again in more ways than one. I want to show Egorr how much I care about him.

I roll over in his lap so I'm facing his chest, then slide down until I'm kneeling between his thighs. Already he's tenting his sweatpants, and they do nothing to hide the massive shape of him underneath.

"Your cock blows my mind," I say, rubbing a hand across it over the fabric. Egorr's nostrils flare.

"You like it?" He sounds uncertain.

I lower my lashes and wrap my hand as far around it as I can, given the barrier between us. "I love it."

He takes a sharp breath and shakes his head, like he doesn't believe me. Egorr's never been shy about his body, but I do get the sense he's a little self-conscious after what he told me. *What beautiful human wants an ogre?*

Well, this one does, for starters. And I'm going to show him just how much.

I loop my fingers in the band of his sweatpants and, taking care with how hard he is, pull them down. Egorr shifts to allow them off, his eyes growing even bigger as I fully expose him to the air, shoving the pants all the way down to his ankles. I drag a hand over his rounded belly to the thick hair between his legs, where that impressive cock of his juts out toward me. The tip is already glistening, and a wicked smile crosses my face.

I'm going to make this ogre moan for me.

I stick my tongue out, licking off that bead of cum, and Egorr gasps. I love how responsive he is to every touch, so I run a finger down the immense length of him, just giving him a taste. His cock twitches under my hand, and when I look up, he's watching me intently, eyes wide.

With a smirk, I wrap my fingers around the thick base of him, and his eyelids flutter. It only takes a few strokes to work him up even more, another droplet of cum spilling out, then another. I smear it all over his cockhead for additional lubrication, roaming up and down him even faster as he rewards me.

"Maddie," Egorr mumbles, his belly tightening and flexing with every pump of my hand. "Ah—that's so good."

I haven't even fucked him with my mouth yet and he's already whimpering my name. Guess it's time to blow his mind.

Pulling his foreskin back, I lean down and sweep my tongue across the soft head of his cock, earning a surprised gasp, then again and again until Egorr's hips are rising up off the couch. I swirl my tongue all around it, licking up each new salty drip he has to offer me.

"Your cock is perfect," I tell him, just before I bring the entire thing between my lips. Egorr opens his mouth to speak, but all that comes out is a moan as I sink him deep into my mouth. Just to really shock him to his core, I relax my throat and continue bringing him in, until he's literally too thick for me to take anymore.

Egorr lets out a heavy breath. "Oh, fuck." I would smile if my mouth weren't full of dick, knowing I made him swear.

Keeping my teeth tucked behind my lips, which is difficult to do when you're trying to deep throat something the size of a water bottle, I slide him back out again, keeping both hands moving. Egorr groans, and I'm immensely pleased at the variety of completely un-self-conscious sounds he's making for me. One of his hands lands on my head, and I pop my lips off his crown.

"You can grab my hair if you want." To encourage him, I give him a wicked smile and slide him in deep again. Egorr doesn't hesitate to bury his fingers in my hair, and then with an almost comical gentleness, he tugs on it, encouraging me onward. Keeping my amusement to myself, I let him move my head in his own rhythm, showing me what speed he likes best.

It's when I drop one of my hands to encircle his balls that Egorr really starts to let loose. He jerks against my mouth, his hand tightening in my hair. With a force I don't think he realizes he's applying, he shoves me back down on his cock, and I manage to tamp down my gag reflex just in time. I work his balls at the same time as the shaft, letting myself fully fall into him, into pleasuring him, into earning those lovely sounds of pleasure from his lips.

That's when I have a wicked idea.

I lean back and pull off his cock, and Egorr raises his head, blinking a few times as if he was in a daze. I scoot up, so my hips are planted firmly between his thighs, then yank off my shirt.

Egorr stares at me. "Maddie?"

Without answering, I shed my bra next, until I'm tits-out in front of him. Then I lean down, and holding my breasts apart, I slide his cock between them.

Egorr's mouth falls open as I squeeze them upward, then down again in a rolling motion, and he's still slick enough that he travels easily through them. Then I tilt my chin down as far as I can and lick the head of his cock.

"You're incredible," Egorr whispers as I lean over him, giving him the boob job of my life. Now he's leaking everywhere, and I love just how much cum he makes for me. I use it to lube him up further. "Oh, fuck, Maddie. Ah!" He's struggling to keep his eyes on me as I pleasure him. "You're so beautiful. I can't believe it."

I squeeze him harder between my breasts. "Believe it."

Slowing down, I bring him into my mouth again, getting

him soaking wet before resuming my boob attack. His lips part, and his head falls back.

"I'm going to come," Egorr grunts, his cock already starting to swell noticeably.

I grin wickedly up at him. "Get it all over me."

He looks down at me right as white liquid bursts out of him, landing squarely on my nose and cheeks. Egorr lets out a gravelly roar as even more gushes out, dripping all over my tits and hands. I stare back at him, cum painting my face, and my tongue darts out to lick some off my nose.

Egorr lies there, panting as if he's just run a marathon. Then, suddenly, I'm swept up into a huge hug, my ogre's massive arms curling tight around me. He pulls me down onto the couch with him, bundling me up so tight I'm almost suffocating against his chest.

"Thank you, little Maddie," he murmurs into my hair, stroking it. "I'm so grateful for you, I can't even express it with words."

"Well," I say against his chest, the words coming out muffled, "I won't mind if you try."

Egorr snorts and pulls me tighter, as if he's trying to make me a part of himself. Eventually, he lets me go free to clean up. But he chuckles when I emerge from the bathroom, and I wonder what he's laughing about.

"You still have some here." Egorr wipes my forehead with his thumb. "I sure got it all over you."

"You're a regular Jackson Pollock."

My ogre guffaws this time, and I sure love making him laugh.

By the time I wake up the next morning, Egorr's already left for work. There's a note for me on the fridge.

"Left some breakfast for you in here," it says. "There should be lots to eat around the house, and I'll bring something home tonight for dinner."

I rifle through the fridge until I find the covered plate with hash browns and sausage, then pop it in the microwave.

After cleaning for most of the morning, I run out of things to do around the house. Maybe it would be all right if I went on a walk—I just need to stretch my legs, even if it's nothing strenuous.

Like the doctor ordered, I think with an eye roll.

I decide to explore Egorr's neighborhood and get a lay of the land. I probably shouldn't venture too far alone in case I come across one of the more dangerous monsters that might live nearby, but a few blocks should be fine.

It's a perfectly beautiful day, the blue sky shining bright in my eyes. I'm enjoying myself, but when I reach the end of the street in just a few minutes, I sigh. I probably shouldn't keep going without Egorr.

But as I turn around to head home, I find myself standing a few dozen yards away from a very, *very* large troll.

She's probably ten feet tall, with a big nose and gray, pock-marked skin that looks to be made of stone. Moss covers her back and shoulders, as if she's been standing in the exact same place for decades.

When she spots me, she freezes. I'm not sure if I should run. Are trolls aggressive? I have no idea.

Shit. Maybe it was a bad idea for me to go out by myself.

"Hello?" the troll calls out, standing in place.

"Um, hi." I keep my distance, and start backing up, just in case. Her eyebrows draw down low.

"Are you all right?" she asks in a concerned tone.

"I'm fine! As long as you, uh, stay over there." After my run-in with the giant, I don't want to put myself in a position to be picked up and eaten again.

"You're alone." The troll looks unhappy about this. "You shouldn't be out alone."

"I'm not," I lie. "My boyfriend is around. He's an ogre."

"Oh!" She brightens at the mention. "Is his name Egorr?"

I blink. "You know him?"

"Yes, yes, of course." She stays where she is, and I'm a little less worried that she's going to cross the distance between us and attack me. "He always comes to the neighborhood meetings. Quiet, but a good guy."

Cautiously, I take a step toward her. The troll smiles, showing off some chipped stone teeth.

"I promise I won't hurt you," she says, holding up her hands. "I'm just worried seeing a human wandering around without protection. What are you doing out here?"

I let out a weary sigh. "It's just boring being inside all day. I thought I'd go out and get some fresh air."

She nods. "Can I escort you?" I get closer, close enough that she can hold out her huge hand. "I'm Timble, by the way."

I finally cross the space between us and clasp her hand. We shake, and her stone skin is cold against my palm.

"I guess an escort would be nice. I want to see more of the neighborhood."

Timble grins and gestures over her shoulder. "Well, there's a road back that way that goes into the next neighborhood. We could walk there. There's a lovely park."

My ears perk up. "A park? That sounds great."

Timble looks excited. "It's about a mile there and back, and the trees are pretty this time of year."

I offer a smile. "All right. Sounds good."

Chapter Twelve

$\mathcal{W}$e walk under falling autumn leaves to the park, and I find out right away that Timble is about as talkative as I am. I tell her about my trial marriage with Egorr, and she asks all sorts of questions about what life was like for me on the preserve.

"Boring," I admit. "It's so much more interesting out here in the world. Meeting a stranger on the street, for example."

Timble laughs. "Normally I'm not out and about on a work-day, but I just got laid off." She sighs as we pass the playground. "So I've got some time on my hands until I can find something else."

"I'm sorry. What do you do for a living?"

"Mental health. Counseling, mostly. It can be a little taxing emotionally, so I'm enjoying my break while I can before I find a new clinic."

"I'd be happy to help you look," I say. "I'm a whiz with a computer."

Timble grins. "Thank you. I'd like that."

We learn all about each other on our walk, and by the time

we reach Egorr's house, I think I've made a friend. There, Timble waves goodbye to me.

"Give me a call soon," she says. "Egorr has my number. Maybe I could have you over for lunch."

That sounds like the perfect thing to occupy my time, so I agree enthusiastically.

When I open the front door, I find the fire is lit inside. Egorr leaps out of his chair at the table the moment I step in, and his eyes are red around the edges.

"Maddie!" He rushes toward me and sweeps me up into his arms. "I was so worried! Where have you been?"

I gasp in his tight grip. "You're home early."

"I wanted to see you." He sets me down, worry etched onto his face. "But you weren't here when I got back."

"I made a friend!" I'm still buzzing from my afternoon. "She was really nice."

"A friend?" His frown deepens. "Who? A monster?"

"Yeah. Her name is Timble."

"My neighbor, the troll?"

"Yep! That one." I twirl in a circle. "We had a lot of fun getting to know each other after she found me out walking."

His brow furrows. "You went out alone?"

"Yeah. I was bored."

Egorr sits down on the couch and rubs his forehead.

"I guess it probably is boring being home all day." He sighs. "But you shouldn't go out by yourself."

"Why not?" I'm a little incensed by his protectiveness. "I was fine."

"This time." He raises his eyes to mine, and I can't mistake the hint of fear in his eyes. "But what about next time?"

Of course I understand his worry. This world isn't friendly to a human like me. I saw that already with the rock giant. But I can't stay inside all the time, either.

"Well, next time I'll be with Timble," I say, grinning as I sink onto the couch next to him, cuddling into his side. "She's unemployed right now and says she has time to spend with me. We went on a long walk."

Egorr chuckles. "That sounds fun." Then he sits down on the couch with a serious look on his face. "But it frightened me, Maddie. I thought you might never come home."

I lean into his shoulder. "I'm sorry for worrying you."

Putting his arm around me, my ogre pulls me in close. "It's all right. But maybe take your phone with you and text me when you go out?"

"Okay. I will."

Egorr kisses my forehead, and I tilt up my chin so he can kiss my mouth, too. I love the way his big lower lip worries mine, gently teasing me open so his tongue can pass inside. I meet it head-on, and soon I'm in Egorr's lap, my legs straddling his waist, his wonderful cock already alert for me. For a moment I wonder if ogre cum is addictive, because I just want to suck him off again.

Suddenly he pulls away, panting. "Wait. I brought home food. It's on the counter."

"Aww," I say, sitting back on his thighs. "But you could feed me something else."

His eyes go wide, and then a huge guffaw bursts out of him. He wraps his arms around me and squashes me against his big body.

"You're wonderful, Maddie," he says, voice full of emotion. "I'm so glad you came home with me."

"And I'm glad you sent in your application," I say, my voice muffled by his big chest.

Eventually we pull apart, and Egorr sets out the boxes of Chinese food he picked up on his way home. The moment we're finished, I grab his hand in mine. Maybe I have to wait for my body to heal for some activities, but there's still a lot we can do in the meantime, and I want to explore everything I can with Egorr.

He follows me to his bedroom, where once again I demand he take off his clothes, and then he takes off mine until we're both naked on the bed—my favorite place to be. I spend time exploring him, kissing from his mouth down his chest to his big belly, and then finally to that huge, swollen cock. I suck him thoroughly, swallowing every drop he gives me.

"My turn," Egorr says, his voice a low growl. "It's all right as long as I don't irritate the injury, right?"

"Um, it should be fine." The doctor didn't say anything about oral being off the table, and I sure wouldn't mind Egorr's face between my legs. "As long as you don't, you know..."

He nods in understanding. "I'll be careful. Now lie down, beautiful."

He's never called me that before, and it makes me blush a little as I fall back into his pillows. Egorr crouches over me, leaning down on his elbows to kiss the tip of my nose, then my lips. I hungrily kiss him back, always eager for his lips on mine. But before it can turn into one of those deep kisses I enjoy, he pulls away. Instead, he trails kisses down my throat to my collarbone, then between the valley of my breasts. He cups both of them in his hands, his lids falling low over his eyes.

"These are amazing," he murmurs, kissing the tip of each of my nipples. My back arches up, seeking even more, and Egorr relents, sucking one up into his mouth. He tugs on it with his lips, plucking it until I'm gasping.

Then he continues on, down my belly to the hidden place between my legs. There, I open them for him, eager for what comes next.

Egorr is gentle at first, gusting his breath over my clit, before he swipes his tongue across it. Ah, that's what I needed.

While he licks at his own slow pace, he reaches up to squeeze one of my breasts, fondling the nipple.

Without vaginal penetration, it takes longer for him to whip me up into a storm, but soon Egorr is licking and sucking my clit with his full attention, driving tendrils of heat all across my body. Moans stream from my mouth, filling up Egorr's bedroom as he lavishes his affection on my pussy.

Then, very abruptly, I hit my crest. I cry out, grabbing Egorr's bare head to steady myself as a massive orgasm rushes through me. I clench up all over, even my legs, which traps him between my thighs.

"Maddie," Egorr groans, his tongue still tormenting me, still demanding more. "You taste so good, I'll never get enough."

Once I've come down, I sit up to kiss him, to tell him how much I appreciate him, but Egorr has a wicked glint in his eye. Staying on his knees, he pushes me down to the bed.

"No." He licks his lips. "I'm going to make you come until you can't anymore."

Oh, don't mind if I do.

Three orgasms later, I'm wrung out like a limp rag. Egorr lies down next to me, kissing my cheek with his adorably wet mouth.

"I could listen to you moan all day," he murmurs to me, bringing me into the circle of his arms. "Maybe this weekend I'll try it out."

I giggle against his chest. "You're going to make me hoarse."

Egorr nuzzles the top of my head. "Then I'll know I've done my job."

As promised, Timble invites me over for lunch the next day. It seems like a good idea until I realize almost everything she eats is some kind of raw plant.

"Oh, sorry," she says, stuffing a dandelion in her mouth. "I honestly didn't know what humans ate."

"That's all right." I watch her suck up a few sprouts. "I wouldn't expect you to."

Even if she doesn't eat the same kind of food that I do, it's good to have a friend, at least. I feel much less alone.

I help her look for jobs that afternoon, but there's not much on the market. Eventually I get a text from Egorr that he's gotten home, and Timble escorts me back to his house.

When I see my ogre again, I jump up and wrap my arms around his neck. With a laugh, he catches me by the butt, my lips crashing into his.

Oh, how I want to try again. I want Egorr in all ways, and as much as sucking his dick has been a lovely distraction in the meantime, I am, frankly, hornier than a billy goat.

I can't stop thinking about it as we cook dinner together, and I wonder if Egorr's thinking the same thing, because he finds every opportunity to touch me as he busies about the kitchen. We eat quietly, but the whole time I'm observing him, admiring his big tusks, his bright eyes, and his big lips.

Fuck. I'm definitely down for the count. Fallen, head over heels. It's been less than a week and I'm beyond infatuated with this big, beefy green guy.

Finally I set my fork down on my plate, a little too hard, and it fills the quiet room with a metallic *clang!* Egorr glances up at me, surprised.

"Maddie? What's up?"

"I..." I swallow hard. "I really like it here, Egorr. And, um... I really like *you*."

There. I've said it. It's not quite as strong of a word as how I feel, but I'm not quite sure if it's love yet, either.

His smile brings his tusks up past his eyes.

"I really like you, too," he says, his hand drifting across the table toward mine. He twines our fingers together, and I grip his tightly. "I've loved having you here."

"And we survived our first fight!" I quip.

Egorr blushes, but nods in agreement. "We did."

"Will you..." I rub my cheek surreptitiously. "Do you want to take a bath with me tonight?" If I have to sit in the water for a while anyway, I'd love not to do it alone.

A wide smile crosses his face. "Of course."

He fills the tub with warm water, then we both climb in together. I sit in the nest of his legs, my butt against his crotch. Though his cock grows thick and hard behind me, Egorr simply holds me, occasionally pouring warm water over my shoulders. As I relax and sink deeper into the bath, he washes my hair, and it's heaven to be under his hands.

Maybe we can't do all the things I'm dying to do, but at least we're together—and I'll relish it so much more when I can finally have my ogre in all the ways I want.

Chapter Thirteen

*T*he days pass much quicker now that I have someone to spend time with. Timble isn't shy at all, which is perfect for me. She's funny and bright, and even makes a few dirty jokes. She lives alone, but that's by choice.

"I'm just not interested," she says with a shrug when I ask whether she's considered marriage herself. "I like having my space, and I don't really need, you know..." She winks. "Sex isn't something I care about, and I've never been much of a romantic, either."

In this way, we are polar opposites, and it's fascinating. She's dated a few times, but finds she prefers spending her time in the company of close friends. One day, we meet up for coffee with one of these friends: a very tall, very clawed harpy with a loud voice. She's a little much for me, but it's clear Timble adores her, and I love how dedicated the troll is to those she cares about.

But as one week turns into two, and I still can't be with Egorr in the way I want, my mood takes a turn. Giving him blowjobs every day, and getting eaten out in return, sates a need in me, sure—but it doesn't take care of all of them, and I've come to detest sitting in the warm water every day just waiting to heal. I try to keep smiling when Egorr is home, but even I can't keep the disappointment off my face when we agree that we shouldn't try out the forging class yet. It'll be too strenuous an activity.

"I'm sorry," Egorr says, bending down low to look into my eyes as they get wet with tears. "I know it's hard." He hugs me tight, but I still feel like he deserves more than I can give him.

Timble has opened up to me a lot since we started spending time together, but I'm still hesitant to tell anyone about my injury. Eventually, though, she notices I haven't spoken much on our walk.

"Are you all right?" Timble asks in that low, soothing voice of hers. "Usually you're all energy."

I bite the inside of my mouth. "I'm fine. Just tired, I guess."

We cross the street, heading toward the park, while Timble crosses her arms behind her back and hums.

"You know, if there's something you want to talk about, you can talk about it with me."

I think it's the first time I've heard her inner therapist peek out.

"Talking won't help," I say with a sigh. "I just have to wait. And I hate waiting."

"What are you waiting for?"

I take a deep breath, because I've been dreading this. "I'm... waiting until Egorr and I can try having sex again."

Timble lowers her head to peer into my face. "Try again? Wait, back up. What do you mean?"

I knew this was coming, and now I have no choice but to tell her the whole story.

Keeping back the gory details, I give an overview—how I rushed us into it, then Egorr took me to the doctor, and now there's still two or more weeks to go until I'm cleared for any funny business.

"Oh, I'm so sorry, Maddie." Timble shoots me a sympathetic look. "That sounds difficult. And painful, too."

I shrug. "It's not as bad now as it was at first. I think the stupid warm water baths are working." As much as I hate to admit it. "But it sucks that it's stalled everything. We were doing so well!" I kick a rock.

"What do you mean? Are you and Egorr not doing well now?" Timble frowns. "I would have expected better of him."

"No, no." I wave my hands to dispel whatever bad thing she's thinking. "I think I'm more upset about it than he is."

Timble looks relieved. "Egorr's a good ogre."

"He really is." I sigh. "Which is why this blows so much. I want to show him how much I like him, but I can't." My face heats as I add, "Outside of giving him tons of blowjobs, I guess."

I love Timble's gravelly laugh. "I imagine he gets the picture."

But does he? No matter how much Egorr assures me that he likes me, that he cares about me with or without sex, I still wonder. I wonder if it's enough for him, if he's going to lose interest before I'm better again.

And even then...

"Maddie?" Timble's giving me a concerned look as we pass under the tree branches, which are now almost bare. The sky is clear but it's chilly out, and I'm glad I brought my thicker coat today.

"It's just that, you know, even when I do heal, we're just going to have the same problem again. Isn't that going to be awkward?" I bunch up my shoulders, trying to keep warm. "I guess I haven't really gotten over what happened at the pub."

Egorr wouldn't have this problem with that ogress we met.

"The pub?" Timble shakes her head. "What happened at the pub?"

I'm still embarrassed by how irrationally I behaved over something so silly, how I put myself in danger and then got so angry at Egorr.

"It's okay," Timble says. "You don't have to tell me if you're not ready."

I shake my head. "It's not that. I was just... stupid. And I don't like to think about it." And yet I can't stop thinking about it. I still worry that one day, Egorr is going to change his mind and send me home, and the likelihood of that happening feels like it's increasing every day that I'm still injured.

Timble frowns and lets out a *hmph*. "Stupid? I don't like it when you're mean to yourself, Maddie. You're my friend, and nobody gets to be mean to my friends."

I laugh because it's a very Timble thing to say.

"But it's true. I got really jealous of this ogress who was hitting on Egorr, and that's ugly." I'm ashamed of myself and how possessive I felt over Egorr. I regret that I ran off.

Timble just smiles at me. "You're in a new relationship, so give yourself some grace. I think you don't fully trust him yet, and that's getting in the way."

It hits me like a truck.

"Maybe I don't." I hate how it sounds. "But it's not about him. It's about me."

But Timble just nods in understanding. "Trust is something that has to be built over time. It doesn't appear by magic." She offers me an encouraging smile. "And you and Egorr are building that together, right now. But trust is also a risk." We stop where the path ends and becomes a city street again, then turn around and head back the way we came. "You were afraid of me when you first saw me. But you took a risk to come and say hello."

That's true. I had to believe she was telling me the truth when she said she knew Egorr. I decided to risk it.

"And now we trust each other more, right?" she asks.

I nod agreeably. I know Timble would never hurt me, and she would make sure no one else did, either.

"Maybe you and Egorr could do some trust building together while you're healing, so when you're ready, you'll have a better foundation."

"You want us to do trust falls?" I say, a little skeptically. "He's too big."

Timble snorts. "No. But there are lots of intimate ways to do it." She waggles her eyebrows. "You could blindfold each other. Explore yourselves and one another in all kinds of new ways."

The idea of blindfolds is like a key in a lock. I turn it, and the door opens, revealing an entire array of activities I'd never considered. I wonder what Egorr would do if I couldn't see him. What would *I* do if he couldn't see me?

"Do you want to go visit Dame Yemi?" Timble asks.

I blink at her. "Dame who?"

"It's a store. They sell all sorts of things like that. You could probably find a dilator or a training kit there, too."

My eyes go huge. "Are you talking about a *sex* store?"

She chuckles. "You could call it that. Maybe go with Egorr and browse. You might get some other ideas, too."

My mouth is watering just thinking about it.

Yes. That's what I want. It would be a fun adventure for us, and maybe it would add some excitement, too, while we're waiting for me to heal.

I can't wait to see Egorr's face when I ask him.

~

As I expected, Egorr turns a dark, dark shade of green when I explain that Timble told me all about Dame Yemi—and I want to go check it out.

"Really?" he says hoarsely. "I've never been inside."

"Well, now's your chance!" I tackled him the moment he came in the door, and he hasn't even had a chance to hang up his keys yet. "Can we go?"

"Sure, all right. We can get something to eat while we're out. But first..." Egorr leans down and curls his hand around my back, his lips widening. "I want to greet you properly."

I'll never get tired of Egorr's kisses. I run a hand up his tusk as he tantalizes my lips, then tugs me closer as our tongues test each other. Soon I'm letting out little noises against him as he crushes me to his body, cupping my ass. My toes leave the floor.

Finally, he sets me back down and pulls away, still blushing.

"I'm kind of excited," Egorr says as we head out to the car. "I've always wondered what's in there."

It's a pleasant drive to the city, and we stop at a burger joint on the way. Egorr has three, and even packs away some fries, too.

Dame Yemi's is a shockingly pink building on a street corner in the city. We have to drive around a while to find a parking spot, then we walk toward it hand in hand. As usual, monsters who notice me stare as we walk by, surprised by the human in their midst.

The store has a bright facade with a glowing sign on it in curly-cue letters. A mannequin in full dominatrix attire stands in the window beside the door, and I pause to stare at it before we step inside.

There's just as much color on the interior of Dame Yemi's as there is black leather. If it's not black, it's rainbow, and I'm immediately enamored with everything. There are wigs, leather harnesses, collars and whips. I pause in the doorway, and I must be staring like a total tourist because somebody laughs behind the counter.

It's a rather large cyclops wearing a leather vest and tight vinyl pants, which allow me a solid eyeful of his butt as he steps out from behind the counter.

"First time?" he asks with a wink.

I grin from ear to ear, but Egorr already looks somewhat mortified.

"Sure is," I say, bouncing forward on my toes.

The cyclops spins an impulse buy stand covered in dildo-shaped keychains. "I don't have much that's human-sized... well, very little, actually. But what are you in the market for?"

"Blindfolds!" I answer immediately. "My therapist friend suggested them."

The cyclops blinks. "Therapist?"

"That's what we're here for?" Egorr rubs his bald head. "I didn't realize there was an agenda."

I grab his arm and pull him into the shop. "It's just one item on the agenda. The rest is whatever we want it to be."

The cyclops snorts as he leads us around the counter toward the hangers of clothing on the wall. There are leather thongs covered in metal studs, bras and jockstraps. Just past them, the cyclops pauses at a rack of masks.

"Here you are." He gestures at a row of blindfolds that come in all sorts of colors. "Your choice."

I let out an *ooh* as I pick through the different colors. Part of me is leaning toward the traditional black, though, so I grab one and hold it up. "Got it."

"I'll take it up to the front for you," the cyclops says, and I hand it over. He leans forward conspiratorially, so I lean forward, too. "Feel free to look around. Take your time. But be sure to check out the back room." With another wink, he points off toward the rear of the store, then returns to the cash register to help the next monster who comes in.

I keep my eye on that back room as Egorr and I browse. The cyclops is right in that most everything is too big for me—but it's not too big for Egorr. I size him up in his work shirt and slacks, imagining him with nothing on save for a leather jockstrap and a collar.

Yeah, I think I'd really, really like that.

Preparing my speech, I gesture to the row of various cups and speedos. But Egorr is already taking one off the rack, arching an eyebrow at me.

"First blindfolds, now these, hmm?" His lip pulls up on one side. "What do you have planned, little Maddie?"

I lick my lips. "Well, I thought it would be fun to try some new things." I pull down one of the collars, too, and boldly hold it up to Egorr's thick neck, as if I'm showing him in a mirror what he'd look like in it.

His good-natured grin turns knowing and smug as he takes the collar and the jockstrap, then leaves them both on the counter for the cyclops to pick up.

I'm still eyeing that back room, so I tug on Egorr's shirt sleeve. "Can we go back there now?" I point toward the open doorway.

"Whatever you want." He loops our arms together. "Let's go explore."

Chapter Fourteen

I don't know what to expect as we head into the "back room," but it's unlike anything I could have imagined.

A sex doll sits high up on a wall, looking down over us with vacant eyes. A glass dildo that's even bigger than Egorr's cock sits on a pedestal to my right, and on my left is a tall rack covered in a dozen kinds of strangely shaped vibrators. I pause in front of them, cocking my head.

"What are these?" I pluck one off the rack and turn it over to read the label. It has one appendage that appears to go inside, and another appendage meant to stimulate the clitoris. "Whoa. Two in one?"

Egorr peers over my shoulder. "That would be fun to play with," he murmurs in my ear. I shiver all over as his hand trails down my back. "You could even play with yourself."

"Would you watch?" I ask.

"Always."

But I want to keep looking around before I make any decisions, so I put the toy back and we continue perusing. There's another end cap with anal plugs in every possible color and size, and shelves full of erotic videos behind it. Those pique my interest. Sure, I've watched porn before, but never *with* someone. The possibilities back here feel utterly endless.

I take Egorr's hand in mine as we reach the end of the videos and arrive at the dildos. I've never seen so many shapes and sizes in my life, and in comparison to me, they all look huge. Many have illustrated monsters on the labels—a dragon with a knobby cock, a werewolf with a massive knot.

"Wow." I pull one of the knotted ones off the hook and hold it up. "Good thing you don't have one of those," I tell Egorr. "That would never fit."

"We could make it fit," he says, biting his lip.

My whole body grows warm looking at them, imagining they're all Egorr's cock, instead.

"Is there anything in particular you're looking for?"

The voice takes me by surprise, and I jump into Egorr's side. He wraps an arm around me as we turn to face the minotaur who seems to have appeared out of nowhere, her hair all shaved on one side. She cocks her head curiously.

"A human!" She crouches down a little to look into my face. "Wow. Haven't seen a human before."

"Hi," I manage, still rattled.

"Sorry to surprise you." She offers me an apologetic smile. "Can I help you find something?"

I glance up at Egorr, suddenly feeling embarrassed. He jumps in to save me.

"Yes, that would be great. We're looking for a, um... something to help with, you know." He gestures at the two of us next to each other. "I'm a little big for her."

The minotaur's eyes widen as she catches his drift. "Oh, I see!" She claps her hands together. "I think I can help. We have many different training kits available."

She hurries off into the racks, so Egorr and I follow along behind her. She locates a box on a shelf and pulls it down to show us. On the front are three silicone toys of varying sizes.

"This is a training kit. You start off small, then work your way up. It has instructions inside to help you." She hands the kit to me so I can read the back. The smallest one looks to be about as thick as a human cock. The biggest one is much closer to Egorr's size. I could probably draw his dick to scale from memory now if I had to.

Once I've looked over the box, I hand it to Egorr.

"We should get it," he says without a second thought.

"Wonderful!" The minotaur takes the box back and grins. "I also recommend toy lube. I can show you some different kinds, they come in lots of flavors."

The minotaur shows us all the options, and I pick strawberry—which I know is Egorr's favorite—before we head back to the front counter.

"Thanks for your help," I say as the minotaur heads back to restocking vibrators. I definitely plan on returning here in the future.

"No problem. Good luck to you and your ogre."

When we're all checked out, I'm humming with excitement to get home and try out our new things. Just imagining Egorr in that leather collar gets me hot and bothered. He shoots me a look as he puts the car in drive that says he's imagining it, too.

The moment we're home and inside the front door, Egorr's arm snakes around my waist and yanks me against him. I'm surprised and pleased by how eager he is to get his hands on me, and I melt against his body, dropping the paper bag in my hand.

He traps my cheeks in his palms, looking down into my eyes with the most intense combination of affection and lust I've ever seen.

"I loved shopping for toys with you," he murmurs, rubbing the tip of his nose against mine. "And I can't wait for what you've got planned."

I rise onto my toes and peck his lips, then stoop down to pick up the bag. I take out the jock strap and the collar, holding them both out. Egorr's brows shoot up.

"Put these on?"

His smug smile widens, and he takes both of them without argument. While he's occupied in the bathroom, I sneak into his bedroom and take off my clothes, then lie on my side on the bed to await Egorr's return.

But I'm not prepared at all for him. When my ogre steps in wearing nothing but a strap around his hips with his heavy cock tucked into the leather pouch, my jaw practically falls off my face. The collar fits perfectly around his thick neck, and all I can do is stand there and stare.

Egorr raises an eyebrow. "What do you think?"

"What do I *think*?" I sit up on the bed on my knees and beckon him closer with one finger. With a smile, he walks toward me until we're nearly face to face, and I smooth my hands from his shoulders down his body, over his full pectorals and broad belly to where the leather is holding him in. I can't wait to take it off him, but I'm going to enjoy the sights first. "I think you're fucking hot. I think I want to touch you all over." I kiss his tusk, then move down to his cheek, his jawline, his throat. Egorr's breath comes faster as I work my way down to the hollow of his collarbone, then to his nipples. Curiously, I take one in my mouth, and his eyes fall closed.

"You like that?" I ask, teasing it with my tongue as it hardens.

"Y-yes." Egorr's body twitches under my attentions, so I switch to the other nipple, giving it the same treatment. His chest is rising and falling faster now. I'm dying to pull that jock-strap off already and sink his cock into my mouth, but I want to take it slow.

When I'm finished teasing him there, I trail my lips down over his belly to where the studded leather strap is clasped around him. Teasingly I brush over the cup with one hand, and Egorr shudders under me.

"Maddie," he murmurs, stroking my hair as he pushes it back from my face. "I want to put the blindfold on you."

I'm surprised by this, but immensely pleased. So he wants me to be his subject, too?

Gamely, I pick up the paper bag and pull out the blindfold we bought, then he helps me put it on, tying it around the back of my head. For the briefest moment, as the world goes dark, my heart speeds up. What is Egorr going to do with me while I can't see him?

"Lie down." Egorr's voice is soft and comforting, and I do as I'm told, falling back against his pillow. "There we are."

The mattress sags as Egorr climbs onto it, and uncon-sciously, my thighs clench closed. Something about the blind-fold has disconnected me from the world, and suddenly, I'm nervous. I know Egorr would never hurt me, but I also don't know what to expect, and that unsettles me.

Soft fingers land on my feet, but all Egorr does is gently massage my toes. His hands work down the arch of my foot, squeezing and rubbing as he goes. I start to relax into his attentions as he works his way up to my ankle, then my calf, smoothing his fingers along the tense muscle.

He doesn't speak at all as he continues, just familiarizing himself with my body. He smooths over my knees, then digs his thumbs into my thighs, which I didn't realize were knotted up until he starts massaging them.

"You're so beautiful," Egorr says under his breath as he works his hands up to my pelvis, where he brushes over the hair there. "I like how you look in everything you wear... but especially without anything covering you."

I sense his body settling down beside me on the bed as his fingers dance over my belly, then up to my ribs. He simply traces the outline of my breasts, and now my nervousness has faded into hunger. I want him to touch them, to tweak my nipples and lick me all over.

"Egorr," I whimper.

But even as I wriggle under his hands, he takes his sweet time, exploring up to my shoulders and down my arms, until he reaches my hands. There, he twines our fingers together, and I feel his hot breath on my face as he leans down.

"Yes, little Maddie?" He lifts my hand and presses it to his chest, where I can feel his big heart beating.

"Please touch me."

I love the sound of his hearty chuckle as he releases me, then glides his fingers up my hip to the swell of my breast. He cups it, testing it, massaging it as I gasp with pleasure. He moves southward, too, his other hand pausing at the crux of my thighs. I spread them open for him and his finger slips down, just to my clit, which he gently brushes. I feel him shift on the bed again, and then his lips latch onto my nipple.

The sensation of everything he's doing is so heightened by the blindfold that I moan. He continues sucking on me, teasing my clit, ramping me up higher and higher. When he's thoroughly loved both my nipples, Egorr kisses his way down my sternum to my belly, and then lower.

When he licks me there, all my nerves are aflame. He goes slow, winding me up at a steady pace, cupping my ass in his hands as he lifts me up even closer to his mouth, carefully avoiding anything below my clit. Soon I'm bucking in his hands, my whole body tensing as he winds me tighter and tighter. Somehow he grabs my nipple while he's eating me out like a champ, plucking it and driving me absolutely wild.

"Egorr!" My thighs clench as my climax erupts, showering me with sparks. I'm shivering as he gently releases me, lowering me back down to the bed. I still can't see a thing, but I don't need to.

I reach out aimlessly until Egorr's hand finds mine. I sit up on the bed, tottering on my unsteady knees, as he shows me where he is. My fingers curl in the hair on his chest, then trace upward to the collar cinched around his neck. I tug on it just enough that Egorr lowers his head, and I kiss him, tasting myself on his lips.

"You're amazing at that," I tell him, falling into his arms.

"It's easy with you. I feel like I know just what your body wants."

But now I have things I want to do, and a certain ogre I want to see.

Chapter Fifteen

When I'm free of the blindfold, I shake my hair out and gaze up at Egorr. He's towering over me on the bed, his cock straining at the jockstrap.

Fuck, that's hot. But I want to tease him first, like he's teased me.

"Sit against the headboard," I say in my bossiest tone. With a playful smirk, Egorr slides backward on the bed until he's reached the pillow. Then I take the blindfold and cover his eyes, tying it behind his head, grinning wickedly the whole time. Once he's bound up, I do what he did to me, and explore him all over. I know his wrist bothers him, so I start with his left hand, massaging his palm and wrist and arm.

Egorr sags forward, his lips parting. "That's incredible."

I continue upward until I reach his chest, where my lips take over from my hands. I kiss down his body, admiring every crease and swell of him, until I get to the strap. His cock is bulging, desperately trying to escape its leather sling. I pet him on top of it until he squirms, his breath coming faster.

"Aw, do you want me to let you out?" I ask, squeezing it. A

moan falls from Egorr's mouth. Instead of indulging him, though, I continue tormenting him over the leather, rubbing my naked breasts against his belly, kissing him everywhere I can reach.

"Maddie," he says breathlessly, bucking up into my hands as I reach underneath and pay attention to his balls, too. "Everything you do feels so good."

Egorr groans the more I rub him, skating my ass over the jockstrap. I love how easy it is to earn a response from him, how willingly he lets me know that he's enjoying himself.

Eventually, feeling sorry for him, I unfasten the buckle and the pressure is relieved, his cock finally springing free. It's thick and heavy, the tip already seeping a thick, white liquid. If anything, it's swollen even more than usual after being confined for so long.

Cupping his huge balls, I kiss from the tip of his cock down the shaft to the base, nuzzling it with my nose as I go. Egorr's head falls back against the headboard with an audible *thump!* as I wrap my hand around the root of his cock and apply firm pressure.

"You're so good at that, Maddie," he says, even though I've barely done anything. Yet.

I kiss my way back to his cockhead, which is now throbbing beneath his foreskin. I slide my tongue inside and lap him up, and his hips tremble under my hands.

I love how powerful he makes me feel, making this massive ogre tremble with just my mouth.

Pushing the skin back, I drag my tongue all around the head like it's the tip of an ice cream cone, licking up each new droplet of cum as it comes out of him. Egorr's panting by the time I wrap my lips around the whole thing, both my hands gripping his shaft.

Then, I go to town. A harsh groan falls from his mouth as I

suck him in deep on my first attempt, then go shallow to tease him. I repeat this, over and over, until he's panting and gasping and his hips are bucking off the bed.

"Maddie," he moans, "that's perfect."

I hollow out my cheeks and suck in as I take as much of him as I can, then slide my tongue along the length of him. Experimenting on him is fun, and it's driving him wild.

Finally, I return to pumping him in and out, playing with his huge balls as I move faster and faster. His breathing ratchets up, and then suddenly his hand is on the back of my head, his fingers in my hair.

He erupts in my mouth, shooting down the back of my throat. I swallow it all down, but there's more coming, and I apply gentle pressure to his sac to get even more out of him. Egorr shudders as he collapses against the headboard, his chest heaving.

I sit up and wipe my lips, grinning like a dork. Egorr tears off the blindfold and pulls me against him, wrapping me up in his arms while I use him as a bed.

"Thank you," he murmurs into my hair. "Thank you so much for being with me. For doing fun, new things with me like this."

I loop my hands around his neck and kiss him. "I'm glad I get to do them with you."

Timble is thrilled when I tell her how it went at Dame Yemi's.

"What a happily ever after!" she crows. "Next thing you know, you'll have Egorr tied to a bedpost at your mercy."

I blink. Oh, I hadn't considered that.

"New item added to the to-do list," I say, checking off an invisible box. "I think I could rock his world."

Egorr works from home the following day, and something about our excursion with the blindfold has unleashed, or perhaps awakened, a new level of sexual chemistry between us. We can't keep our hands off each other as we go about our day, and on his "lunch break," Egorr surprises me by aggressively leading me back to the bedroom.

"I know what I want to eat," he says in a low voice, shoving the door open. Then he pushes me down to the bed and devours me like I'm his last meal on earth until I'm writhing and squeezing his big head between my thighs.

Before I can return the favor, Egorr's out the door again, rushing to get on a conference call. As he slips on his headset, I kiss him on the cheek.

"Can't wait to suck your dick later," I whisper, and his eyes go huge as he covers the microphone. Giggling, I skitter away to the kitchen to make myself a sandwich.

That night, we make a quick frozen dinner, then hurry back to Egorr's bedroom. I feel more comfortable with him now than I ever have before. I've gotten to know his whole body with the help of the blindfold, just as he's gotten to know mine.

And I learn something new about him every day. He loves video games, but has prioritized spending time with me since I moved in.

"Show me!" I demand one night. "I want to play with you."

His face alights. "Really? You want to play?"

"Of course." I want to do everything with him, but I don't say that part. A girl needs to have some secrets, after all.

We take up residence on the couch together, and Egorr puts a controller in my hand.

"Have you played a lot of games before?"

I shake my head. "A couple of phone games, but that's it."

"Got it." He shows me what each of the buttons does and then turns on the game. It's a racing game, where we get to pick our own carts and even customize them. I don't know which driver to choose, but Egorr finds me a good "beginner" option.

I have a feeling he's going to wreck me, but I'm up for it.

When the game starts, I'm completely out of my element. I do manage to finish the first course, though I'm in last place.

"Just let me get the hang of it," I say. "Then I'll destroy you."

Egorr guffaws. "Let's see you try."

I didn't know he was a shit-talker, but it just makes me like him even more. There are so many different sides to Egorr, and the more of them I learn, the more I find myself falling for him.

That's what's happening, I know it. My heart is crazy about him, wanting more looks and more touches every day.

I do a bit better on the second course, and even manage to beat one of the computer players set to "easy" mode. Egorr comes in first place, of course, absolutely decimating the competition. For the next round, he turns on hard mode for himself, which should even us out. I pout a little that he's putting himself at a disadvantage, but it does mean we come in second and third place, respectively.

"You'll get better at it the more you play," Egorr says after we've blasted through another few rounds. "You're already catching up to me!"

I peck him on the cheek. "That's sweet, but let's see how it goes when we're both playing on the same difficulty."

"You don't want an easy win, do you?" He puts an arm around me on the couch, pulling me into his side. I snuggle against his big chest.

"No. It's better if you have to work for it." I wiggle my butt to show what I mean, and Egorr chuckles. His hand trails down my side, brushing my boobs, and I run my own fingers over his belly to the growing lump under his sweatpants.

Then it's off to his bedroom, where Egorr puts on his collar and lets me have my way with him long into the night.

On Thursday, we go to one of the neighborhood meetings together. After the routine business of mowed lawns and late trash pickup is covered, Egorr introduces me to some of the other monsters that live nearby—a dragon who resides in a cave at the end of the street, and his next-door neighbors, a pair of dwarves who are not all that small. In fact, they tower over me, both of them as broad as a house, and I'm mystified by this.

"I thought the whole thing about dwarves is that they're short," I whisper to Egorr.

He cocks his head quizzically. "You sure learned some strange things on the preserve. Like your whole obsession with delivery pizza."

I blow out my cheeks like a chipmunk. "Are you making fun of me?"

"I think it's cute." He leans down to kiss the top of my head. "But I guess I am making fun of you. A little bit."

It's clear everyone in the neighborhood respects Egorr, even though he's sometimes awkward and doesn't know what to say, and I adore that about him.

The longer we go about our daily lives together, the more comfortable and happy I feel. We still sleep in our separate bedrooms, which is one of my sticking points. Though life is good and easy together, I still wonder how this will all end. There's no time limit to a trial marriage, but Egorr hasn't proposed to me, either. I'm nervous about getting too close, enmeshing our lives too deeply, in case it doesn't work out in the long term.

The more time passes, though, the more just the thought of

it brings tears to my eyes. I can't imagine life without Egorr anymore, but it's still a possibility this could all end with me going home.

I just hope that he decides he wants me to stay—forever.

I continue taking the warm water baths for another two weeks. Then one morning, I check the calendar that Egorr keeps hanging in the hallway, and find that today has been circled in blue marker.

It's been one month since that fateful night. We can finally try again.

I'm bouncing up and down by the time Egorr gets home. I don't think he realizes what day it is as he steps in the door like he usually does after work, and I practically throw myself at him.

"Egorr! Guess what, guess what?"

He blinks down at me. "What?"

"I'm healed! I think."

He doesn't look as happy as I expected him to, though.

"We should schedule another doctor's appointment so we can be sure," he says, a note of caution in his voice.

I falter. "Really? But everything feels good."

Egorr wraps an arm around me and hugs me against his side. "I know. But... Maddie." When he releases me, he kneels in front of me and takes both my hands in his. "I never want to hurt you again. That was the worst day of my life, knowing I'd done that to you."

I look down into his earnest face and immediately my impatience and frustration drains away. He's so good—almost too good.

"Fine." I pout. "But can we go to the doctor soon?"

"I'll call right now."

Egorr sets an appointment, but it's not for two more days, which feels like an eternity to me. Then he invites me to sit on the couch and we play a few rounds of Blast Karts together, until we can't keep our hands off of each other anymore, and I strip off Egorr's pants right there. When he comes, he paints my face and neck, and he hastily apologizes for getting it all over me. I laugh, then take off my own clothes and invite him to take a shower together.

Under the hot water, Egorr pulls my naked body against his and holds me tight.

"I can't wait to use the training kit," he says, stroking my wet hair.

I wiggle, squeezing my breasts against him. "Yeah? So you can fuck me?"

He hums. "That's right. We're going to work you up to my cock." Egorr leans down. "And then I'll fuck you so many times you'll beg me to stop."

I shiver all over at the thought.

Chapter Sixteen

$\mathcal{I}$t's the longest two days of my life, but finally the afternoon of our appointment arrives. I can't seem to stop talking, too excited about my checkup to slow down. Egorr chuckles when we arrive at the office and I let out a little squeal.

"I've never seen someone so excited to go to the doctor before," he muses, opening the door for me.

When we're finally in the exam room, we're attended by the faun once again.

"Good to see you." She sits on her stool and brings out my chart. "Almost exactly four weeks. How do you feel?"

"Couldn't be better," I chirp. "Everything feels great."

The faun laughs at my enthusiasm. She pulls up the hospital gown and peers between my legs with a flashlight. It's uncomfortable, but I can tolerate this again if it means I get to go home with Egorr and play afterward.

"Oh, it's looking good down here." The doctor checks me out a few moments longer before wheeling her stool away.

"Yup. I think you're all healed. You must have taken good care of it."

I grin, even though it was a pain in the ass. "Sure did."

With the doc's seal of approval, I'm more eager than ever to get in the car and head back. I practically drag Egorr out through the waiting room to the car, then I dive into the passenger seat. He has a wide, silly grin on his face as he buckles himself in and pulls out of the parking lot.

It's the longest drive ever, and I keep sneaking glances at Egorr. He has a big smile on his face, too, and occasionally his eyes flick over to me before going back to the road.

Then, at last, we're there, and I jump out of the car and run for it before remembering I need to close the car door behind me first.

Once we're inside, it's only three in the afternoon so there's no dinner to get in the way. I'm about to sprint down the hall when Egorr bends down and scoops me up into his arms like I weigh nothing.

I hold on to him by the neck and giggle as he practically jogs to his room. There he skids and turns, and now I'm laughing as he tosses me onto the bed. With a springiness that surprises me given his size, Egorr hops onto it and crouches over me.

"Are you ready?" he asks, letting his hips lower and brush over mine. "For me to play with that pretty pussy of yours until it can take me?"

Just the promise of it makes me moan. "Yes!"

I thought we'd strip ourselves down like we usually do, but this time Egorr's the one who pulls off my shirt, then unhooks my bra, throwing it away without a second look. The moment my tits are out, he's latched onto them, sliding an arm under my back to bring me even closer to his mouth.

I love eager Egorr.

While he laps me up hungrily, his hand trails down to my jeans, where he rubs me between the legs. But I need more than that, so I quickly unbutton them, then slide down the zipper. Egorr breaks away from tormenting my nipples long enough to shuck off my jeans, but when I try to pull down his own pants, he stops me.

"This is about you," he says, tapping me on the nose. "I'm going to worship every single inch of you."

I wiggle underneath him, thrilled by the promise.

"And you had better do what I say," he says, lowering his voice. He pushes me down harder against the bed, his hand traveling from my breast up to my wrist, which he gently tugs toward my other wrist, until he's gripping both of them. I light up all over, surprised by this turn of events.

Egorr wants to tell me what to do? All my nerve endings light up. Yes, please.

I lift my hips to grind my bare pelvis against his clothed one, rubbing that big lump in his sweatpants.

"All right," I say, wiggling to create friction. "Whatever you say."

He smirks a rather self-satisfied smirk, and I think I like this Egorr, the one who's confident and dominant. I know he wants me, more than anything, and that fills me up with a cozy warmth.

"Now, keep your arms up here." Egorr releases me, instead using his hands to push my thighs apart, until I'm spread out wantonly in front of him. He licks his lips, spreading his middle and index finger to drag them down the lips of my pussy.

"Look at you." His voice is lower, quieter, full of adoration. "So beautiful everywhere." He kisses along the inside of my thigh, getting closer and closer to where I want him. "You smell so good here."

Wow, no one's ever said that to me before. It's hot.

"Really?" I ask.

"It's *you*," he says, by way of explanation. Then he licks me with the long flat of his wide tongue, all the way from my seam to my clit. There at the top, he stops and swirls that incredible tongue around, reaching under my ass while he eats me to squeeze one cheek in his huge palm.

"And you taste fucking delicious, too." Egorr grunts with pleasure as he licks me up faster and faster, and he's already mastered my body because soon I'm racing around the corner, toward the finish line.

Then, a gentle finger prods me lower down. Egorr lets out a groan as he presses between my lower lips, finding me wet. That finger explores farther, and I welcome him in.

"Oh, fuck, that feels good." My head falls back on the pillow. How I've *needed* that. The additional stimulation that just this taste of him provides nearly sends me catapulting into an orgasm.

Then he wades deeper, and I'm shivering all over, wildly sensitive from a whole month of no stimulation there at all. Now his finger is gently, slowly pumping inside me, and Egorr is still licking and sucking me like a champ.

But right before I'm about to leap into the unknown and let it swallow me up, Egorr slows his movements down.

"Why are you stopping?" I whimper, sitting up.

Egorr sits back. "Stay here," he says, instead of answering. When he reaches over to the bedside table, the training kit is waiting, each of the three toys inside it unpackaged and cleaned.

Wow, he prepared for this. He was just as optimistic as I was about the doctor's visit, and he's also as eager as I am to work toward our goal.

Egorr spreads my legs, then kneels between them, the toy gripped in his big hand. Gosh, it looks like nothing in comparison to his cock, even though he still has it hidden in his pants. The toy should fit easily, right?

"Are you ready?" he asks, peering up at me.

"I'm ready." More than ready.

With a nod, he pours out lube into his hand, then caresses the toy with it, turning it shiny. Licking his lips, he bends down between my legs, brushing his tongue over my clit. It only takes a few seconds of him licking and sucking on me for my pussy to start craving something inside it.

As if he can read my mind, Egorr gently presses the tip of the toy between my folds, the angled head guiding it through. Oh, that feels even better than his finger.

I collapse back to the bed, taken over by the sensation of just this one sample. Egorr rocks the toy back and forth, going deeper a little at a time before pulling back out again. It feels easy and natural, if a little cold, but I'm quickly warming it up.

Then Egorr leans down and, never slowing his attack with the toy, starts licking me again.

I let out a wild cry, because the feeling of the toy and Egorr's mouth has me back where I was only moments ago. I open wider and the toy pushes deeper, and now my hips are bucking up into his grip, and Egorr is fucking my clit with his tongue so fast that I'm curling and tensing and every neuron in my brain is firing all at once—

"Fuck!" I scream it as the toy pushes in all the way, and Egorr's talented tongue destroys me. I arch my whole body up, my spine shaking with the sheer power of my climax. I feel like I'm being broken apart and then put back together again in shivering pieces.

When I'm finally back down flat on the bed, my chest heaving with exertion, Egorr sits back and wipes his face with his wrist.

"Wow," he says with a self-satisfied grin. "Haven't heard

you scream like that yet." He gently works the toy free of me, and it's dripping. "Can't wait to make you scream even more with my cock."

An extra tremble ripples through me at the suggestion.

He sets the toy aside, and we both glance at the second one on the bedside table. I took the first one easily, so surely I can take the bigger one, too.

I want to be ready for him. I want to take the next step.

"Can we try it?" I ask.

Egorr arches a brow. "Are you sure?"

"We can stop if it doesn't fit." But now that I've experienced the power of Egorr's mouth with the toy inside me once... I'm hooked.

He gives an uncertain nod, then picks up the second toy. I fall back down to the bed, wriggling with anticipation as he covers it with lube, then returns to his position between my legs. He teases my clit with his thumb, and even though I just had one of the most incredible orgasms of my life, my body is eager and ready for more.

This time, the head of the toy asks me to open for it. Egorr twists it as he gently pushes the toy in, spreading the lube around, which makes it shockingly easy for it to fit. I close my eyes at the onslaught, willing myself to relax and accept it.

Then the shock of Egorr's tongue on me returns, and I let out a strangled moan as he presses the toy deeper. It's stretching me wide, almost too wide but not quite. And oh, how damned good it feels. My thighs tense as Egorr keeps it shallow, thrusting in and out with the toy while he flicks my clit from side to side.

"Fuck, please, more," I whimper, wanting to be filled as fully as possible. With a pleased grin, he gives me what I want, sliding even more of that cool length inside me. My hips rise into it, eager to swallow it up. Egorr's mouth moves faster, circling and suck-ing, while he pumps the toy in a regular, thoroughly wondrous rhythm. The stretch is delicious and perfect, and just imagining that it will soon be Egorr inside me, I'm already near my finish.

"You're so beautiful," Egorr says as he reaches down with his free hand to rub himself through his pants. "I love the sounds you make, Maddie."

"I want to see you," I manage to say as he continues thrusting the toy inside me. Leaving his due diligence for just a moment, Egorr unbuttons and pulls off his pants, taking his underwear with them, so now that thick cock of his is exposed. My mouth waters as he drags his hand from the root to the tip, a bead of white forming at the slit there.

Then he returns to his work, moving the toy in and out of me at the same pace that he's stroking himself. I'm keening, the toy stimulating every last inch of me while Egorr licks faster, and soon I'm so close to the edge I think my body might simply burst apart.

"Oh, Egorr, oh," the words are streaming out of my mouth against my will, just a string of begging nonsense.

"Faster?" he asks, giving me a mischievous smirk from between my legs as he starts fucking me with the toy at an even more punishing pace.

I can't take it any longer. The bliss of his tongue, the toy, his hand around his cock, all winds together and I erupt like a pile of fireworks. Stars explode in front of my eyes, so bright I'm nearly blinded, and even I'm startled by the shriek that comes out of me. Suddenly the toy feels much too big, the stretch too intoxicating, and I pant, "Please, take it out!"

Hurriedly, Egorr withdraws it, and I collapse to the bed in a pile of spent mush. Egorr tosses the toy aside with the first one, and crawls up the bed to lie down next to me. I can barely take a full breath, my lungs shuddering as I try to return to Earth again.

"Wow," I mutter in a daze. I roll over so I can face Egorr and take his cheeks in my hands. He's grinning like an idiot, too, and I lean up to kiss him, wrapping my hands around his big tusks. He kisses me back with a tenderness that makes me want to cry.

"I loved seeing that toy inside you," he murmurs, nuzzling my nose with his. "And soon it will be me."

Oh, that can't come soon enough.

While we lie there looking into each other's eyes, I trace my hand down his belly to his cock, which is still alert and hard between us. I give him a slow, intentional hand job, smearing his cum around as it leaks out the tip. Soon he's the one panting and shivering under me as I bring him closer and closer, taking my sweet time. I love how he loses himself in the pleasure, gripping my arm tight in his huge hand as his hips rock in time with my movements.

"Thank you," I say in a quiet voice as he moans. "Thank you for taking such good care with me, Egorr. Thank you for everything."

And then, he goes rigid, and cum shoots out in a waterfall, painting me from my breasts to my belly. Egorr lets out an immense sigh of contentment and pulls me in close, even though I'm covered in him.

"Always," he says, kissing the top of my head and then resting his cheek against it. "I'll always take care of you, Maddie."

Chapter Seventeen

*A*fter our afternoon escapade with the toys, Egorr and I are both reluctant to get out of bed—until his stomach grumbles, and we admit it's about time to make dinner.

Tomorrow is Saturday, though, which means we get to spend the whole day together. Even better, Egorr already has an activity planned: going on a hike into the hills behind his home. There are only a few good days left before winter comes, and he wants to make the best of it.

"We might see deer, rabbits, foxes, maybe even a bear," he says as we start chopping vegetables and meat together.

I glance up from the cutting board. "I bet you could take on a bear."

Egorr snorts. "I think I could, too. But I doubt I'll ever have to."

The thought reminds me of how glad I am to be here, out in the world and beyond the walls of New Eden, where there are plenty of places to explore and wildlife to see. This is what I wanted when I first went to live with Shisek, and now I finally have it.

The next morning, there's a chilly breeze in the air when we head off into the woods, but once we're surrounded by trees, I feel safe and warm. Egorr holds my small hand in his big palm as we hike up the hill, deeper into the state park. It's not long before I spot a big yellow mushroom growing out of a gash in a tree trunk.

"Whoa!" I crouch down to inspect it. "Is this dangerous? I feel like mushrooms are dangerous."

Egorr laughs. "Some of them are, and you definitely shouldn't taste one without knowing for certain first."

"Can you eat this one?"

He leans down to get a closer look. "I think that's a Chicken of the Woods. But I don't have my handbook with me."

I shake my head, giggling to myself. Of course he has a handbook for mushrooms.

"There are all kinds of things you can forage in these woods," Egorr explains as we walk onward.

"Like, things you can cook with?"

"Sure. All the vegetables we eat now started as wild plants." He pauses for a moment, like he has something else to say but isn't sure whether he can.

"What is it, Egorr?" I prompt.

"In the spring, there are lots of wild onions and garlic out here." He rubs his bald head through his beanie. "They're great for cooking with. We could... we could go foraging together."

I smile, because I understand his hesitation at discussing where we might be next year. We have no way of knowing now if we'll get that far.

"That would be fun," I say, deciding I should just go for it. "This has been a lovely hike, and I wonder how different things would look in the spring."

A wide smile spreads across Egorr's face, and I love how it draws up his big tusks. I want to kiss him again—and do even more things with him. As we walk on, his hand grazes over my lower back and I shiver all over, imagining what we'll get up to later.

~

I'm rather cold by the time we return home, and Egorr makes us each a warm cup of hot cocoa. But I'm already dying to get back in the bedroom and take the next step.

This time, we both get naked together, and I revel in the sight of him. Once we're on the bed, Egorr pulls out the blindfold.

"Put this on," he says in that bossy voice from yesterday, and it makes me tingle at the base of my hips.

With a grin, I take the blindfold and cover my eyes, tying it around the back of my head.

"Now lean back," Egorr tells me.

I do as I'm told, all the hair on my skin standing up on end at just the tone of his voice. I lie there like a doll as my ogre begins kissing me, starting with my mouth and then working his way down. I accept all his attentions eagerly, shivering as he tastes my nipples, then my belly. His hand slides between my thighs and he rubs my clit, telling me without words how he's going to pleasure me.

First, he eats me out like it's his last day on Earth, using all his wondrous knowledge of my body to get me spinning faster and faster. Then, one of his fingers slides into me, and he pumps it in and out until I'm chanting his name and begging for more.

With a chuckle, Egorr pushes in a second finger. His pace

ratchets up, and I'm so hypersensitive that I'm letting out little cries with every thrust.

Then he pauses, and I hear the *click!* of the bottle of lube opening. Not being able to see what he's doing makes my heart beat even faster. Is the biggest of the toys going to fit?

"It's going to be a little cold," Egorr says. "Keep your legs spread for me."

Keeping my thighs parted, I jump a little when the cool toy starts to push inside me. I take the head easily, moaning as it slowly slides in.

But then it keeps going. And going. It's so broad that I squeak and reach out for Egorr, and he stops right away.

"Too much?" he asks.

I nod rapidly, too overwhelmed to even speak properly.

Egorr withdraws the toy, then eases it back in less deeply, so only the head is seated inside me. My nerve endings are all white-hot, and I feel like I'm already so close as it stretches me. Then he tries again, pressing the toy through, and this time some more of it fits.

"There you go," Egorr croons. "It looks so amazing inside you, spreading that pussy open for me."

I gasp as his wet tongue glances across my clit, and the toy glides in even deeper. I don't realize it's all the way inside me until it bottoms out.

Then, Egorr really starts to fuck me with it. I'm crying and moaning as he pumps the toy faster, holding my thighs down to the bed while he ravages me with his mouth.

"Come for me, Maddie," Egorr growls, shoving the toy in deep and back out again. He resumes feasting, and I feel like all my seams are going to burst apart.

When I climax, it's as if I'm trapped in an earthquake. My thighs freeze up and my voice stops in my throat, all while the toy continues pumping. I clench so tight that it feels immense, impossible.

"Yes," Egorr praises. "Look at you, gushing all over the toy."

He slows down as I fall flat on my back, heaving with exertion. With the utmost gentleness, he slides it out of me. I sense him crawl up the bed until the mattress sags under him, then he pushes some hair back from my sweaty forehead.

"Fuck," I murmur as the cataclysm slowly washes away. "That was amazing."

He chuckles that deep chuckle I love as I reach up to untie the blindfold. I blink a few times at the bright light overhead.

"You were amazing," Egorr says, running a hand from my collarbone down to my belly, as if he wants to touch as much of me as possible. "Your pussy took that toy so well... I think you're ready now."

A bolt of thrill rushes through me, and I sit up abruptly. "You think we could?" I ask, vibrating with excitement. "Now?"

Egorr sits up, too, and pulls me into his lap so his cock is wedged neatly between the cheeks of my ass. I rub against it, desperate to feel even more of him.

"We should give you a night to recover," he says, kissing the back of my neck. "And then we can do everything you want."

I swoon at the thought. We're almost there.

Sunday is a long day, awaiting what's coming. After sleeping in and then having brunch, we play five rounds of Blast Karts, and for once, I manage to beat Egorr and the computer players both. Then we tidy up the house together before cooking dinner. I make it all the way through our meal before I can't stand the anticipation any longer.

Setting down my fork and napkin, I get up out of my chair and hold out a hand to Egorr. "Can we go to your room?"

He takes it, grinning at me widely. "I'd love to."

Once he's up on his feet and rising high above me, though, he swoops down and picks me up. I squeal as he bridal carries me down the hall, and before long I'm down on his bed on my back, Egorr ravishing my mouth with his. His hand ducks under my shirt and squeezes my breast over my bra, and I'm impressed by how hard he is already as his hips rub eagerly against mine.

"Shirt," he says, in that commanding tone, "off."

"Oh, yes, sir."

He lets me sit up and pry it over my arms, then I unhook my bra. His eyes drop to my tits and he licks his lips.

I love that I can turn my ogre on so much.

"You next," I say, and Egorr gets a particularly mischievous look as he lifts off his T-shirt. I sure do love looking at him without it. Curly black hairs trail all the way from his throat to his crotch, fanning out across his big pecs, which are each twice as big as one of my hands. I can't help touching him, exploring him with my fingers from his collar down to his strong hips. There, I tug on the band of his pants, and he doesn't have to be told twice to take them off.

There it is. His cock comes out, hard and eager, already leaking. My prize. I don't hesitate before leaning down to lick just the tip of it, and Egorr gasps.

"I thought you wanted me to fuck you?" he asks as I trace the head of his cock with my tongue.

"I need dessert. Then after you fill up my belly, you can put it inside me. Okay?"

I think I've finally managed to scandalize him, because Egorr's mouth opens in surprise. I grin as I take his cock deep into my throat on my first try, and he moans.

"Wait," he says suddenly. I pause, and he gestures for me to come toward him. "You'd best put that sweet pussy where I can get my own dessert, too."

Oh, is that what he wants? Happily, I navigate so I'm kneeling astride his face, those big tusks keeping my thighs spread for him. He wraps his hands around my ass, pulling me in even closer before he sets to devouring me, sampling my clit and then diving down again to my entrance, moaning as he licks up all my arousal.

Once more, I wrap my lips around that incredible cock, stretching my mouth as far as I can as I bring it in deep. The head strikes the back of my throat, and yet I swallow it even deeper, angling my neck so I can take as much as possible. Egorr groans as his hips jerk against me.

I go slow, savoring him as he delves deep into me with his tongue, then draws it out and circles my tender nub again. Fuck, I'm so close to coming already. So I speed up my mouth, gripping his cock tight in my fingers while I bring him in as far as I can.

"Oh, Maddie," Egorr whimpers, and I don't think I've ever heard him *whimper*. "You feel incredible. And you taste even better."

He licks me more furiously, and then I sense one of his fingers trail up to my pussy. Just the tip tests me out, and as turned on as I am, I easily give to him. His breaths speed up as he presses it inside me, twisting it this way and that to open me up. For a moment, my mouth halts because I'm so distracted by the loveliness of just that one finger curling to brush my inner walls. I moan against his cock, and Egorr moans in return at the sensation of it. It's like our pleasure is a circle, building and building the more each of us gives to the other.

I return to my work, stroking him with every suck. Soon

Egorr slides another finger inside me, pausing briefly before I rock my hips against it.

"More," I demand, though the words are muffled by the object in my mouth. In response, he pumps his hand faster, both fingers now running along the inside of me.

My orgasm is on top of me before I realize what's happening. I cry out as it sucks me under, and I try desperately to keep blowing him, but it's almost too much for me to bear. I pull out Egorr's cock and gasp raggedly as one ripple of bliss after another echoes through my body.

"Maddie," Egorr growls, seizing me by the hips. "Lie on your back."

Oh, fuck, that sounds good. I do as I'm told, rolling off of him to land on the bed. For such a big beast, Egorr sure does move fast as he climbs on top of me, pinning my arms down and straddling my hips with his thighs. That cock is dripping wet and pointed straight at me.

"Don't move," he says, releasing my hands. I'm too turned on to even speak as his hand slides lower, testing out my oversensitive parts. I wriggle as he fits two fingers inside me once again, but he won't let me escape. Instead, he attempts to slide a third finger in, and my body instantly rejects it.

"Shh," he says quietly, kissing my lips. The dominating force gives way to a loving one as he brushes my forehead with his. He spreads his two fingers, urging my small cavern open, twisting them and applying gentle pressure. Soon, the third slips inside me, and I'm stretched almost as far as I can go.

"There we are." Once again, Egorr kisses me. It's a long, slow, wonderful kiss that makes me feel cherished and desired —everything I've always craved. He continues working me with all three fingers, widening me more and more. "You're going to be so ready for my cock," he tells me, those soft eyes of his boring into mine.

"I am," I say, wriggling my hips to show exactly how much I want it. "Please."

He leans down, bringing his lips right to my ear. "If she begs so sweetly... then I suppose I had better give it to her."

Chapter Eighteen

*E*gorr withdraws his hand, licking each of his fingers, which is wildly erotic. Then he leans back and reaches into the bedside table, producing a bottle of lube. That cock of his is even harder and more alert than before, swelled up dark with blood. He pours the lube into his palm, and I watch in fascination as he coats his entire length with it. Then, after a moment's thought, he applies some to his fingers and spreads it around my pussy, too.

Now there's no way he won't fit.

"Are you ready to take me, little Maddie?" Egorr falls forward on one hand so his huge body is crouched over me, his belly brushing mine. Looking down between us, he fists himself tight and guides it to the spot between my legs that's hungering for him.

"I'm more than ready." I wiggle my hips, trying to bring us closer together, because all I need in this entire universe is my ogre inside me.

Egorr circles my entrance with his soft cockhead, testing it, applying only a small amount of pressure. I moan at just this faint presence, how it's already urging me open. He's taking it slow and careful, pushing in only a hair's breadth at a time, but there's no pain at all—nothing but a steady, glorious stretch as he pushes in. His cock is a little thicker than the toy we used last night, but it feels like heaven. Egorr's wonderfully warm, so firm and yet giving in exactly the right way. There's no resistance as he slides in.

Egorr's arm shakes under him, and he squeezes his eyes shut. "You feel so good. So wet and soft for me."

I can't even utter a word as he withdraws again, then that head slips in deeper, unhindered. My body parts for it, begging for the rest of him, but he slows before going in any farther.

"Egorr, please," I manage to say. I reach up for him, running my hands down his chest to his belly, peeking down at where he's already sheathed part of the way inside me.

Egorr obliges, giving me another inch before pulling back out. But I need more, and more. He grins down at me, nudging my nose with his.

"Soon." His next thrust invades deeper, and thanks to all that lube, my pussy welcomes him. I'm stretching wide, so wide that I can't even clench. It's like every fold of me is unfurling, giving him even more space as he delves in once again. My hips snap up of their own accord, desperate to have all of him.

"Maddie," Egorr says hoarsely. "You're incredible."

But I want cock, not words. I wrap my legs around his hips, digging my heels into his ass, and Egorr lets out a strangled moan as he slides the rest of the way in.

I cry out as he fills me up as far as he possibly can, until my cup is brimming over. My sweet ogre falls down onto both hands, taking halting breaths. I squeeze around him, so stuffed that I have no choice.

"I'm about to go off," Egorr rasps. I hold him there, stroking one of his huge tusks from base to tip. As our bodies adjust to one another, he kisses me, savoring my lips, tangling his tongue with mine. When it looks like he's regained his composure, Egorr slowly pulls back out, and I whimper again with loss.

He plunges into me, hard.

"Egorr!" I grip his tusk hard. "Fuck!"

He pauses, blinking. "Did I hurt you?"

"No!" I moan and clench him even tighter with my thighs. "Please, more! Harder! Faster!"

A wicked look spreads across his face as he repeats the motion, withdrawing most of the way and then shoving himself back inside me again. The sound that comes out of me is somewhere between a scream and a mewl. I've never needed someone as much as I need him.

Egorr maintains this same pace, taking me deeply, slowly, as my body rearranges for him. Soon he can fit even more of himself inside me, and I can't comprehend how much of him there is.

"Your pussy is so perfect," Egorr whispers, kissing my cheek, then reaching down to graze his hand over my nipple. "Like you were made to fit me."

"I was," I moan. "I was."

My arms find their way around his neck, pulling him in even closer, molding my body to his. I need all of him. In answer, Egorr cups the back of my head, bringing me against his shoulder while his other hand hooks under my ass. My thighs spread wider around his girth, my legs now slung up over his hips, and suddenly I can feel even more of him.

"Egorr!" I bury my face in his neck. "Just like that, please, oh!"

My ogre sinks deeper as I open up for him, and pleasure ripples out from the place we're connected, spiraling up from my abdomen to my chest and into my throat. My whole body is tensing, and Egorr groans into my ear.

"You feel so fucking good," he mutters, his tusks brushing my face. "I can't believe it."

"Believe it, baby." I stroke his bald head. "That pussy is all yours."

He groans at my words, and his thrusts speed up, sending out bigger and bigger sparks. I'm writhing and crying out his name over and over as my need swirls up huge and monstrous. I feel like a boat about to capsize, thrown side to side by each wave as it hits me.

"Egorr!" I'm so close to a perilously gargantuan orgasm that I could almost reach out and grasp it. "Fuck me harder!"

He obeys without question, rising to a kneeling position so he can pump his hips in a brutal rhythm. Each stroke triggers another wave, then another, until my boat is about to topple over.

"Ah, Maddie, I'm going to—" Egorr bites his lip, gripping my thighs tight as he shoves that incredible cock into me over and over. His eyes search out mine, and there's so much soft affection in them that I almost can't bear it.

I love this ogre, I know for certain. All I can do is hope that he feels the same way about me.

Then, my climax hits. I scream, my legs trapping Egorr's hips like a vise. He moans raggedly as he continues fucking me, smashing through my orgasm. I grip him tight, digging my nails into his arms and sobbing out his name.

When his cock swells up even larger, Egorr lets out a roar that's more animal than human. It's like every atom is imploding, consuming me as he fucks me into the bed. A wave of hot liquid spills out of him, filling me up, squelching with his last few hard thrusts. Egorr buries himself deep one last time, his fingers digging into my flesh.

Panting above me, my ogre collapses. The overwhelming weight of him eventually brings me back down to earth, and I let out a sound of distress as my lungs compress. Realizing he's crushing me, Egorr rolls to the side, keeping my thighs locked around his waist so we don't have to separate.

"Sorry," he says, his face thoroughly flushed. He gazes at me with something I can only describe as adoration. "That was incredible, Maddie. You're wonderful. So wonderful."

"So are you." I run my hand over his big head, down his pointed ear to his long tusk. At last, I feel like I'm where I belong. "Thank you."

When his cock has softened, he gently slips free of me, and I'm shocked by the amount of cum that gushes out. Egorr quickly goes to the bathroom and returns with a towel to mop it all up. He gets a good look at me between the legs, concern furrowing his brow.

"I'm fine," I tell him, urging him to lie down next to me. "I'll be a little sore, but I'm fine."

He exhales a relieved breath as he settles on the bed and pulls me into his arms.

"Will you sleep here with me tonight?" Egorr asks, kissing down the side of my face as he squeezes me tight against him. I don't think he'd let me go.

I smile into his chest. "Of course. Tonight and any other night you want."

I feel him freeze, and I wonder if I've said something wrong, something presumptuous. But then he lets out a deep, relieved sigh and tucks my head under his chin.

"I want it every night," he says quietly, almost shyly. "Every night, forever."

I'm so stunned by this admission that I don't say anything at first. Then I pull away and tilt up my face to look at him, and there's a worried expression on his face.

"Forever?" I ask, my voice trembling. I don't usually fall

apart like this, but I wonder if I might simply shatter into a hundred pieces. "You really want that? You want *me*?"

Egorr blinks at me, perplexed. "Of course I do. Do you... do you want me?"

Fuck. This big ogre. I throw my arms around him, burying my face in his neck. Tentatively, he returns the embrace.

"I do. I really, really do." Tears prick at the corners of my eyes, and I rub them off on his skin. "You're making me cry, Egorr."

His chest rumbles with a laugh, and he pats the back of my head.

"Sleep for now," he murmurs into my hair. "We'll talk about it more in the morning."

I curl up tight by his side as he brings the blankets over us, and we fall asleep, his big body wrapped around mine.

Chapter Nineteen

---

*T*he next morning, I wake up to a rather massive boner between my ass cheeks. Egorr hums into my hair, and I can feel his big heart beating faster as I grind my hips against his. It doesn't take much for me to tilt forward on the bed and his cock to slide between my legs, and he groans when he finds me already wet there.

Unlike last night, it's easy for him to slip inside me, and he grips my hips tight in his hands as he fills me up. Before long, he's panting and thrusting feverishly.

"Get on your knees," Egorr commands, and my skin prickles all over. Once I'm up on my hands and knees, he fucks me hard from behind.

"Please," I say, bucking against him with every stroke. "Slap my ass." I want to know I'm his. I want to belong to him completely.

With a grunt of approval, Egorr delivers a slap with his big hand, and I moan as it sends a shudder of pleasure through my body. He gasps.

"Oh, you like that?" he asks mischievously. "Your whole pussy tightened up."

"I do," I moan. "I do."

He fucks me until I'm shivering, my arms collapsed on the bed and my ass up in the air, my skin stinging in the most wonderful way.

"Fill me up, please," I beg, almost at my breaking point. I reach down to run my finger over my clit because otherwise, my budding orgasm might consume me alive.

Egorr makes a noise that's almost a snarl as the sensation makes all my muscles clench.

"Yes," he grunts. "Touch yourself, Maddie. Come around me."

So I do, frantically fingering myself while he fucks me harder and harder. What sends me over the edge is Egorr's moan as his cock fattens up inside me, and he sinks deeper than ever, his huge balls slapping my hand with each thrust.

Like some kind of magic trick, we come at the same time, the sound of our pleasure mingling in the air. He thrusts hard once more, filling me up, until his hot cum is dripping down my thighs.

When he slides out of me, Egorr sweeps me up into his arms and carries me to the shower.

"We'd best get you cleaned up," he says with a smirk.

I giggle. "Aren't you going to be late for work?"

"Fuck 'em."

After a thorough, rather sexy shower, he does eventually leave for work, but not before pulling me into his arms so he can kiss me, hard and firm. On his way out the door, I swat his perfect butt.

"You're taking me out to dinner tonight," I say. "We have some matters to discuss."

With an arched eyebrow and a silly grin, Egorr nods agree-ably and heads off to work.

~

I put on my cutest dress, a pair of heels, and even my favorite gold earrings. Then I curl my hair and sweep it up into an intentionally messy bun with ringlets trailing down. I'm waiting at the table when Egorr comes home, and he freezes at the door when he sees me.

"Oh, wow." He takes a few steps toward me like he's not sure he believes it. "You're hot."

I flick a curl over my shoulder and grin. "So are you. Now get dressed, I'm starving!"

With a kiss on my forehead, Egorr quickly changes into something fancier, too, and then we're off.

I'm impatient to start our conversation. We shared some sweet words last night, but I want to know what it all really means—if he's saying what I think he's saying. So the moment our wine is poured and our orders are taken by the two-headed dragon in a suit and tie, I reach across the table and take Egorr's hand.

"I want you to be as clear and straightforward with me as possible," I say.

Egorr furrows his brow. "Of course."

"Do you want to get married?" My voice sounds a little less confident than I intended. "Like, for real?"

He blinks, then tilts his head. "Yes? I meant everything I said last night, Maddie. I want a life with you. Forever. I love you."

I take a few deep breaths so I don't cry again. Egorr looks worried. "Good. Okay. Because... because I love you, too." I inhale sharply. "And I wanted to make sure you meant it."

"Is that what you want, too?"

"Yes!" I bring my voice down when a few other patrons turn to stare at us. "Yes, I absolutely do." Then I lean forward to whisper. "But just so you know, I do have more clothes. We're going to need at least one more dresser."

The smile on Egorr's face is the biggest smile I've ever seen. He gets up out of his chair, then kneels in front of me. Everyone in the restaurant turns to stare, and I can feel when my entire face blooms with red.

"What are you doing?" I whisper.

He shakes his head and shushes me. Then he reaches inside his blazer and pulls out... a box. It's black velvet, and already I know what he's going to do.

"Aw, shit," I say, and the tears break free. "Yes!"

"I didn't even ask yet," Egorr says with a hearty chuckle. He clicks open the box and inside is the cutest damn ring I've ever seen. It has a pink diamond in the middle in a heart shape. Absolutely the cheesiest, most adorable thing he could have bought, and I love him so much for it.

He knows me. He really knows me.

"Will you be my wife, Maddie?" Egorr asks.

Instead of answering, I throw myself at him, knocking over one of the wineglasses. I ignore it completely as I embrace my ogre, kissing up the side of his big, bare head.

"Absolutely." I pull away and quirk one eyebrow at him. "But you don't have a last name. Does that make me Mrs. Egorr?"

He blinks. "Oh. Hmm. It can, if you want."

I laugh as the waiter comes over to clean up, and I just want Egorr to take me home and fuck me madly again, but I know we have to eat first.

He slips the ring on my finger, and I kiss him with my whole heart.

We're like eager, horny teenagers when we get home, our hands exploring each other with wild abandon before we're even in the front door. Egorr strips off my underwear, and then his own pants, but before he can boss me around, I push him down to the couch.

"Oh?" he asks curiously. He has a wily smirk on his face as I climb up onto his lap, still wearing my dress. I push his cock down between us and slide my pussy along it, getting him good and wet, and teasing my own clit with the head. Egorr's eyes roll back as I grind myself against him, getting wetter and more worked up.

"Yes, little Maddie," Egorr groans. "Use me. Take me how you want me."

Slinging my arms over his shoulders to balance myself, I sit up on my knees and bring him in between them, fitting him right where he needs to be. Egorr cups my ass in his hands as I slide down.

I don't think I'll ever get tired of how it feels to join with him again, to feel his big heart beating inside me. Everything is right where it should be—now with bonus engagement ring.

"I can't believe—" I lift myself up, then sink down again, taking even more of him this time. "—you're going to be my husband."

Egorr's eyes widen, and then he squeezes my ass even tighter. "I am. And you're going to be my wife."

I tighten up at his words, and Egorr hums thoughtfully.

"My wife, who I'm going to fuck like this every day," he says, leaning closer as I raise myself up again. "My wife, who will live in my home and sleep in my bed. Forever."

I kiss him feverishly, continuing my frantic, hungry movements. But my thighs are tiring out.

"I don't know how you do this," I say pathetically. "I need to work on my quads."

Egorr laughs, then, keeping us still engaged at the hip, flips me over so I'm on my back on the couch.

Then he really goes at me, thrusting into me at a frenetic pace. It's just what I need, until Egorr reaches down to run his thumb over my clit.

I go from five to one hundred in a few seconds, a surprise climax hitting me square in the face. I moan and clench and desperately grab onto him, but he doesn't relent.

"I know you can come again," he murmurs playfully, slowing his thrusts but making them deeper, more intentional. Now he's rubbing against that place inside me that sends shivers of pleasure up my spine, and it isn't long before I'm shaking and clamoring nonsense.

When another orgasm hits me, Egorr groans. "Yes, Maddie, choke my cock." His eyes fall closed as he buries himself once more, and we crest at the same time. Warm cum fills me up, spilling out down my ass.

"Oh, shit, the couch!"

I reach under me to halt the flow as Egorr swiftly withdraws, then runs to the kitchen to grab a paper towel. We're both laughing as we mop it up, then he fetches fabric cleaner.

After our escapade, we have a little more wine, which leads to even more lecherous touching. After Egorr's had his way with me again in bed, we lie next to each other in the dim light of the bedside lamp.

"Remember those forging classes we talked about?" I ask, stroking one of Egorr's tusks.

"I do."

"What if we went and made our own rings? Wouldn't that be fun? I've heard of people doing that."

He nods. "I like it. Let's do it. I'd love to get to make your wedding band. Though I can't promise it'll be elegant."

I kiss his nose. "If it's from you, I don't care what it looks like."

~

The next day, Egorr encourages me to move the house around any way I want—even suggesting where my dresser (and my future additional dresser) could go.

"And think about when you want to have the wedding," he asks casually as he slips out the door. "Talk it over with Celeste."

I blink, and then he's gone.

Of course, I call Celeste immediately to tell her the news. When the video call starts, the first thing I do is flash my big pink ring in front of the camera.

"Look!" I gush. "Look!"

"I'm looking," Celeste answers. "Is that a ring? He put a ring on you?!"

We both burst out into excited giggles. I tell her all about knocking the wine over, and I describe our current sex life as, "If I could get pregnant, I'd be pregnant."

Celeste snorts into her hand. "He seems like a good fit for you. I'm excited to meet him. When do we pick out your dress?"

We talk over when I should have the wedding, and settle on early September, gambling for weather that's not too hot and not too cold.

As soon as I'm off the phone, I send Timble a message asking her to get coffee. She had an interview today for a new job, and I hope we can celebrate two successes at the same time.

I must be exuding some new kind of "fiancé" energy, because the moment Timble sees me, she quirks a brow and surveys me from head to toe.

"You look different."

I flash the ring. "Egorr asked me to marry him!"

She squeals, and I squeal, and then we hug.

"I knew you two could figure it out," she says as we walk to the coffee shop. "I think you're exactly what Egorr needed—and he's what you needed, too."

And I think that she's right.

Epilogue

Planning a wedding is no joke. There are a million details to keep track of, and my mom has way too many opinions when all I want is to keep it simple and sweet. Celeste plays referee, keeping her at bay and distracting her with simple choices like decorations and napkin colors. Egorr and I spend most of our time deciding what kind of cake we should have, and testing out a variety of different flavors.

Celeste, Timble, and I all go dress shopping together, which is an interesting adventure out in the world for Celeste. After I've chosen a satin number with rhinestones trailing down the seams—and a rather low neckline—a tall gorgon takes my measurements. Everyone is thrilled about what I chose.

"Egorr will fall over dead when he sees you," Timble says, adjusting the train.

Egorr's dad, Ogorr, comes down on a long weekend to visit and meet me for the first time. As I suspected, he's just like Egorr: a big, lovable beast with even bigger tusks.

"They keep growing," Ogorr says when I remark on it,

tapping his finger on the point. "My dad's were as high as his ears by the time he died."

Huh. Learn something new every day. I wonder what Egorr will look like when he's Ogorr's age.

Ogorr stays in my old bedroom, which has now become our guest room slash office, with some of my extra dresses stashed in the closet. Ogorr smiles when he sees them all.

"You're a sweet young lady," he says to me while Egorr cooks food out in the kitchen. "And I can tell my son is head over heels for you."

I rub my cheek. "I hope so, because I'm head over heels for him."

"I noticed." Ogorr grins wide and toothy, just like Egorr does. "I can see the stars in your eyes when you look at each other."

Am I really that obvious? Maybe it's not that surprising. I feel like Egorr has a glow about him, some intangible force drawing me in closer at all times. And I sure do love him more than I ever thought possible.

I come up behind my ogre while he's cooking and run a hand over his taut butt. "What are you making for us?" I ask, wrapping my arms around him from behind—well, as far as they can go, anyway.

He pauses his stirring to lean into me. "Pasta Bolognese! I thought both of you would like it."

I squeeze him even tighter. "That sounds delicious. I can't wait."

"Break it up!" Ogorr calls jokingly from the bar counter. "The wedding isn't for a few more weeks!"

Egorr guffaws and brings me under his arm as he continues stirring. I love watching the two of them, big gentle giants with hearts of gold.

After Ogorr goes to bed, we stay up reading in front of the

fire. Then we trundle off to our bedroom, and Egorr makes love to me as quietly as he can.

~

At last, it's the day of the wedding. Ogorr is there on Egorr's side, along with some monsters he works with and people from our own neighborhood, while my parents, Celeste, and our friend Rob all sit on my side. Timble joins them, and I'm so happy to see all my friends and loved ones in a single place, together.

After the ceremony is over, which we kept short and sweet, the rest of the night is for eating, drinking, and dancing. Egorr isn't much of a dancer, but I insisted that we get a teacher and practice, so we're able to twirl about to the pace of the music without stepping too badly on each other's feet. Egorr's favorite move is when he picks me up and spins me around, and it earns hoots and claps from the crowd.

Then everyone joins us on the dance floor, and we all twirl the night away. There are gifts and toasts, and most of us drink too much. Ogorr nearly crushes my mother when the two of them dance and he loses his balance.

When it's starting to get late, I hug my friends goodbye, and my mom gets teary-eyed.

"I'm so happy you're happy, but I'm sad that you won't be coming home to New Eden again," she says, pushing some hair away from my eyes, which I'm sure are smeared with mascara from all the sweating and happy tears. "But Egorr is perfect for you, and I know you'll have the life you always dreamed about with him."

My dad echoes her, and I start crying as I hug them both. And then, Egorr and I hop into his car, on which my friends have lovingly painted the words HAPPY WEDDING and JUST MARRIED.

As we pull away, the tin cans strung onto the bumper rattle and clang, following us all the way back to our house in the hill.

Finally, we're home. While I stand in the mirror, pulling all the myriad pins out of my hair, Egorr approaches me from behind. He leans down so his chin rests on my head and his arms are hooked around my waist.

"You looked so beautiful tonight," he murmurs, kissing the shell of my ear. "Like a goddess. I can't believe that you're mine."

A shiver of thrill spreads down my arms and legs.

"I am yours," I whisper back, leaning into his arms. "All yours. To do with as you please."

Mischief takes over my sweet ogre's face. His hands traverse up my body, over my dress, exploring every curve and swell of me.

"I love you, Maddie." He splays his hand across my belly. "I couldn't have asked for a more lovely, sweet, and gorgeous wife."

"Don't make me cry again tonight," I say, wiping my face and smearing my makeup even more. "I love you, too. So much it feels like it's too big for my body to hold."

Egorr chuckles as he starts to unfasten the many buttons keeping my dress on. "You are so full of love, and it's one of my favorite things about you."

The dress falls away as he makes his way down to my hips. I shimmy out of it until I'm in nothing but my lacy underwear. Then I turn around and slide Egorr's black jacket off, which makes his big shoulders look even bigger. His shirt goes next, revealing his perfect, hairy chest to me. Then I take off his belt and push his slacks down over his delightful ass. His cock is already at half-mast when it's finally exposed, and all I want to do is worship it.

"Maddie," Egorr says in a warning tone, before I can get down to my knees. "I want you to get on the bed and open your legs for me."

I love when he gets bossy because it usually means he's about to fuck me into oblivion. I climb onto the bed as ordered, and lean back against the headboard, spreading my thighs wide. The bed sinks as Egorr settles between them, and he licks his lips.

"I'm going to get you so wet," he says in a low baritone. Then he attacks me between the legs, knowing exactly how to get me riled up for him. He squeezes his fingers inside me, pumping them in rhythm with his tongue, until I'm so close to climaxing that I'm trembling all over.

But before I can reach my peak, Egorr pulls away. Now his cock is fat and hard for me, and he settles with my knees hooked over his hips.

"My wonderful wife," he says, leaning down to kiss me as he gently pushes inside me. My body has conformed to his shape, and I'm awash with relief as he slides in deep, settling into his seat. Egorr lets out an erotic groan. "You feel so damned good. I can't get enough of this pussy."

He sits back so he can rub his thumb over my clit, and I instantly tighten around him. His eyes roll back in his head as he thrusts again, and he got me so riled up that I almost come right then. All it takes is a few strokes for me to tumble right off the edge, and I scream out loud as Egorr fucks me through it with even, measured pumps. Even as I moan and clench, he keeps teasing my clit.

"I know you have more for me," he says, his grin revealing all of his white teeth and pushing his tusks up to his eyes.

I nod fervently as he fucks me harder, deeper, that lovely

cockhead of his triggering a bolt of sensation every time it passes through me. Soon I can tell that Egorr's holding back his own orgasm, his eyes closed as he concentrates. I'm writhing, lifting my hips so I can take even more of him, crying out his name with every plunge.

"Oh, fuck," Egorr moans, and I sense him filling up, ready to burst. "I'm going to stuff this pussy so full of me."

That's all it takes to send me flying again. I grip him tight around the neck, holding on for dear life as a lightning bolt of pleasure overtakes me.

"Yes, little wife." Egorr buries himself in me one final time, then his warm cum gushes so hot and fast that I can feel it coating me, spilling out in a waterfall. Still sunk in me, he reaches for the roll of toilet paper we keep by the side of the bed, managing to catch most of it before it gets on the comforter.

I giggle, keeping my hips elevated until he's mopped it all up, then I collapse into the blankets. After tossing it all in the trash, Egorr settles beside me, his arm slung across me.

"That was wonderful, *husband*," I croon, nuzzling the side of his face and stroking one of his tusks.

He beams at me. "And we get to do it for the rest of our lives."

"Mmm. I like how that sounds."

We decide on a rather epic honeymoon, where we'll travel the world for a month, taking in all the sights we can and trying every possible kind of food. It's everything I've always dreamed of, visiting the very places I thought I would only ever see on the television and experiencing them for myself. Plus, doing all of it at Egorr's side? It's as magical as it could possibly be. We walk the streets of big cities hand in hand, browsing markets, trying street food, and occasionally buying silly trinkets to put on our refrigerator back home.

I know traveling is not an ogre's favorite thing, as much as he loves his home, but he's willing to do it for me.

By the time we've reached week three, though, I'm ready to be back in our little house, and Egorr is more than ready. At the end of the day, we're both homebodies.

When at last we've returned, I could practically hug our front door.

"Good to be home," Egorr says with a sigh, putting an arm around my shoulders. "It was a wonderful adventure, but now I want to start the rest of my life with you."

My ogre. I couldn't have chosen anyone better for me.

We sit in front of the fire together, and it's cozy and warm in the blankets on the rug now that winter is coming on. Egorr slowly removes my shirt, and then my bra. I wiggle out of my pants, because I love nothing more than getting naked with him, and toss them away. Egorr chuckles as he follows suit, then gently pushes me down to the floor, settling his big weight on top of me.

"Little Maddie." He caresses my cheek. "Thank you. Thank you for accepting me as I am, and helping me get better every day. Thank you for showing me what a big, wonderful, loving heart you have."

"It's all yours, big guy," I tell him, cheekily darting up to kiss his nose.

"I know once I made you doubt how I feel about you." His brow creases as he remembers it. "I want that to never happen again. And I'm going to devote my life to showing you how much I love you."

My chest constricts as he gazes into my eyes, and I wrap my

arms around his neck, pulling him in close for a hug. I nuzzle his bald head, wrapping my legs around his hips.

"You show me every day."

Now his cock is wedged between my thighs, and I move my hips to glide my sex along his shaft. Egorr lets out a huff of air, and kisses my throat, nipping gently with his teeth.

He prepares me slowly, urging the flames of my need higher and higher. When I've already come around his hand twice, and his mouth is wet with me, he rises up and grips me by the hips, lifting them into the air. His cock easily finds its way inside me, back to where we both know it's meant to be.

I moan with contentment as he slides in deep, and Egorr hovers there, merely rocking back and forth. When I'm used to him, open and ready for him, he withdraws, and then plunges in again.

He fucks me with abandon, clutching my thighs around his waist and pinning my hands above my head. My cries fill our little home while he owns me, his movements growing wilder. He slaps my ass, hard, and I scream with bliss.

"Yes, Maddie," he grunts as I get closer and closer, all my muscles straining from how near I am to splitting apart. "Come for me, little wife."

I cry out as it strikes me like a bolt of lightning. Egorr groans, chanting, "Yes, yes, give me everything." Then he moans as I clasp him tight, and he shoves his cock in as far as he can. I can feel when he lets go because warmth fills me, and it immediately spills out everywhere, just like always.

We lie by the fire a while longer after making love, Egorr stroking my hair while I tangle my fingers in the hair on his chest.

"What do you think of making another trip to Dame Yemi's?" he asks in a sleepy voice, and I turn to him, surprised.

"Oh? I would love it."

He grins. "Thought so. I love how easy it is to make you come when I slap your ass. I wonder how turned on you'd get if we did even more?"

"More?" I grin, wriggling in his arms at the suggestion. "What if you tied me up? Or... what if I tied *you* up?"

Egorr's cock twitches against my thigh.

"I think I'd like that," he murmurs in my ear.

It's only when I awaken in Egorr's arms that I realize I've fallen asleep. He carries me into our bedroom and tucks me under the covers, then slides in beside me. I curl up against his perfectly warm, soft body, right where I was always meant to be.

~

Thank you for reading!

I hope you enjoyed Maddie and Egorr's love story. If you did, please consider leaving a review! Reviews help indie authors like me find new readers.

Join My Newsletter!

For all the latest regarding books, and to get a FREE novella that takes place in the Trollkin Lovers universe, sign up for my newsletter!

www.LyonneRiley.com

Acknowledgments

First off, I'd like to thank my Patrons, who came along with me on Maddie and Egorr's journey. You made this book possible!

I would also like to thank everyone involved in helping me through the process of putting out this book. I can't say enough how much I appreciate the help and encouragement of the people around me. Thank you to Rowan Woodcock, who created this amazing cover artwork, and Ash Raven for designing it. To my critique partners: You all make this possible. And of course, I have to thank my amazing spouse, who has always supported my dreams—and given me lots of inspiration for my characters' sexy adventures.

I couldn't have done this without the expertise of my fellow self-published romance authors. Thank you for inviting me into your circles and helping me through this process.

And thank you to my readers, who gave this book a shot.

About the Author

Lyonne Riley published her first book at age five, which was written on tiny sheets of notebook paper, and she insisted on giving a copy to everyone she knew. She's been writing ever since, from fan fiction in her teen years to original fiction as an adult. After a stint in traditional publishing, she discovered what she truly wanted to write: very smutty stories about monsters and the little humans they worship.

Now she lives in the middle of nowhere with her dogs and spouse, writing sexy fairy tales.

www.ingramcontent.com/pod-product-compliance
Lightning Source LLC
Chambersburg PA
CBHW060605190726
48283CB00003B/1158